MARKED FOR MURDER

"I decided to give the room a second time over and that's when I turned up the small notebook under the phone. I didn't know whether it was left behind on purpose or not, but it told me what I wanted to know. Max the Ax had been staying here.

"When I opened the small, blue covered spiral notebook, what I saw on the first page froze me solid. There were three addresses written down. One was mine, one was the office address, and the other — well, the other one was the one that scared me and made me sure that this had been the Ax's room.

"The third address was Julie's!"

EYE IN THE RING

Robert J. Randisi

PaperJacks LTD.

TORONTO   NEW YORK

PaperJacks

EYE IN THE RING

PaperJacks LTD

330 STEELCASE RD. E., MARKHAM, ONT. L3R 2M1
210 FIFTH AVE., NEW YORK, N.Y. 10010

PaperJacks edition published October 1987

ISBN 0-7701-0646-3
Copyright © 1982 by Robert J. Randisi
Printed in the USA

This one is for Anna and Christopher,
in recognition of their patience and
understanding.

And for my favorite TV
eyes: Harry Orwell, David
Ross, John McGill and
Thomas Magnum.

And for Dominick, who knew how to end
it and how to sell it.

CHAPTER ONE

My left eye had fallen out of my head and was rolling around on the canvas somewhere. I hoped that neither I nor my opponent would step on it and squish it. They were doing wonders reattaching loose parts these days.

Actually, it hadn't really fallen out, but for all the good it was doing me in that ring at the time, it might just as well have. The simple truth of the matter was that it was the eighth round of a ten-round fight and my opponent's jab—he was a southpaw—had been working on that eye for so long that the damned thing had closed up tight on me and I was fighting half blind.

When the bell ending the eighth round sounded I groped my way back to my corner and sat down heavily on my stool. My brother hopped into the ring and began working on me. The ring doctor leaned over and took a look at my eye.

"If it was earlier in the fight, I'd stop it right now," he told us and the referee, who was also inspecting my eye now.

"You can't stop it now," my brother Benny yelled at them.

Why not? I almost asked, but Benny would never have forgiven me.

Both men backed away, and when I knew they couldn't hear me I asked Benny, "Is it cut?"

"No, it ain't cut," he told me, "but it's shut tight. You want me to stop it?"

"Shit no," I said, which was just what he wanted to hear.

1

"I've got him right where I want him; now all I have to do is find where that is. Point me in the right direction, will you?"

"Listen, somebody in the fifth row noticed something," he told me, leaning closer to me.

"I'm losing?"

"Shut up and listen, will ya? When he jabs he drops his left. You got that?"

"Yeah, jabs, drops left. So?"

I knew that already, I just hadn't been able to tee off in time to capitalize on it. That was my problem the whole night, more than anything else. I just couldn't seem to get off, get started.

"Well, here's something else. When he jabs you, count one-two, just like that, and then throw your right and follow with a left. Have you got that?"

I took a mouthful of water, spit it out and nodded.

"Say it!" he insisted, vigorously rubbing my arms and chest.

"Okay, okay, I count one-two, just like that, throw right and follow with left. Benny?"

"What?"

"You seen my eye anywhere?"

The buzzer sounded and he said, "Just don't forget to count, okay? We'll buy you a new eye out of the purse!" He got out of the ring and I stood, waiting for the bell. When it rang I ran out to the center of the ring, right into another jab. It jarred me and sent my mouthpiece to the canvas.

My opponent was taller than me, and he had a longer reach; but I was still determined to be the aggressor, as I usually was in my fights. Sometimes you can swing a round, just my being aggressive.

I bore in on him, and he threw that damned jab again, catching me flush on the eye. It split then, I knew it split, and the blood started to run down my face. I knew if I didn't catch him this round, the doc and the ref wouldn't let me come out for the tenth.

"Count, damn it!" I heard Benny yell. I said, "Shit," to myself, and he threw the jab again. I counted one-two and threw my right. It caught him right on the cheek, and I was so shocked that I forgot to throw the follow-up left.

"The left, the left!" Benny was yelling, sounding like a crazy man, which I sometimes thought he was.

I bore in again, took the jab, counted, and threw the right-left combo. They both landed and shook the guy up. Every time he threw that jab, I nailed him again, right-left. I started

2

swinging harder and harder. I had to get to him before they stopped the fight because of my cut.

I spit out the blood that was flowing into my mouth and bulled him into his own corner. He threw a weak, defensive jab now, all the snap gone from it, and I swung from the heels, first the right, then the left. His knees sagged, and I swung again, right, then left, then the right, then the left...

He fell down as I was throwing a hard right, and I missed and almost went down on top of him. The crowd was screaming and yelling, and the ref pushed me away to a neutral corner. I staggered to it and waited while he counted, "... eight...nine...ten."

It was over.

My brother was in the ring, saying, "Can you hear me? Can you see me?" He was holding a towel tightly to my cut eye, so how the fuck could I see him, I wanted to ask.

"I won," I told him proudly. "I won the fuckin' fight!"

"No shit," he said.

They moved me to the center of the ring, and the ring announcer was shouting into his microphone, "The winner by a knockout—Kid Jacoby!"

CHAPTER TWO

The next morning my face hurt like hell.

The eye was not as swollen, but it was still half shut—and it had taken twelve stiches to close the gash. I had never gotten so marked up during a fight before, but then I had never fought a southpaw before, either.

When I shaved I tried not to look at my face, so as a result I cut myself twice—like I could spare the blood, right?

As I was dressing the phone rang.

"Jack?" a voice asked. It was Eddie Waters, the guy I worked for part-time, when I wasn't fighting.

"Yeah, Eddie?"

"Today's the day, Jack. You comin' in?"

That surprised me. Today was the day, huh. I had forgotten all about it.

"I'll be in after breakfast, Eddie. Thanks."

I had the same breakfast I always have the day after a fight: steak, eggs, hash browns, coffee, toast and grapefruit juice. After that I went to Eddie's office at Fifth Avenue and Forty-ninth Street.

His office was on the fifth floor, and the lettering on the door said Waters Investigations. Underneath that it said Edward F. Waters.

I had been working part-time for Eddie for the past three years. Today was my third anniversary. It was also the day I qualified for a license of my own, which had been the whole purpose of working for Eddie in the first place.

I walked right in.

"You won?" Missy asked as I entered. Her tone said plainly that I didn't look the way a winner is supposed to look.

"Hard to believe, huh? Is Eddie in?"

"Yeah, he's been waiting for you."

Missy had been Eddie's secretary and Gal Friday for the past five years. She was about twenty-eight now and still as pretty as an eighteen-year-old. Red hair, green eyes and a body that won't stop. It won't start either—with me, anyway. Lord knows I tried often enough, but she says she doesn't like fighters. Florists are more her speed. At least, the guy she was seeing now was a florist.

No accounting for taste.

I walked into Eddie's office after a quick here-I-come knock on the door.

"Hi, Jack. Congrats on another stylish win," he said, smiling broadly.

"I ain't pretty, but I gets the job done," I told him in a pug voice.

"Seriously, what's your record now?" he asked.

"Twelve and two," I told him. I needed that win last night. After starting out ten and oh in my first ten fights, I had now split my last four bouts. My style had cost me two bouts, because I'm a brawler and two boxers had beaten me on points. After last night's debacle, I was going to have to give some serious thought to a change of styles.

"I gotta admire you, Miles. I didn't think you'd last as long as you have."

Eddie had always felt that I started too late to make anything of myself in the fight game. Three years ago I had started working for him the same week I had my first fight. I was twenty-four. Most fighters have been fighting ten years by the time they reach that age. Twenty-four is old to start any sport; but I'd had fourteen fights up until this point, and I hadn't lost one until earlier this year. I followed that with a knockout win, then lost again on a split decision. I followed that by taking on that southpaw last night. I won that fight, but I had help.

Somebody in the fifth row.

"Here," Eddie said, handing me a brown business-size envelope. I opened it and took out my brand-new private investigator's license.

6

"I jumped the gun a little," he confessed, "so I'd have it for you today. I filled in the hours on your application and submitted it." He extended his hand and said, "Welcome to the club."

I shook his hand and put the license in my pocket.

"You don't look overjoyed," he observed.

"I guess three years of process serving, tail jobs and runaway husbands have sort of dampened my enthusiasm."

"I told you in the beginning that it wasn't a glamour racket, Miles." He only called me "Miles" when he was dead serious, otherwise, as with most people I was friendly with, he called me "Jack." As a rule, only people who didn't know me well call me by my proper name, with the exceptions of Benny and his wife, Julie. Benny has always called me Miles, since we were kids, and Julie calls me Miles because it kind of keeps a space between us and reminds us that we are sister and brother-in-law.

"I know, I remember," I said, replying to his remark.

Eddie was about forty-five, now. He'd been a cop for ten years before going out on his own. Now he was a private investigator and had been for fourteen years. He still enjoyed the racket. He was his own man, and that had been what he was after he left the department. His hair was starting to thin out now, but his face was the same, open and trusting. It was his greatest weapon.

We had met through a mutual friend, and I had mentioned wanting to get into his game. He agreed to take me on for the required three years so I could get my license. After that, he said, we'd talk.

Now it was time, and I didn't want to talk. Not just yet. I wasn't ready.

I touched my wallet where my license now reposed and thought, Now that you've got it, what are you going to do with it? The same could be said for my record as a fighter. Now that I was 12–2, what could I do with it?

Suddenly, I felt very depressed. I was twenty-seven, and what was I going to do with my life?

One of my goals had been to open my own office once I got my license.

The other had been to become middleweight champ.

Which one took precedence?

Maybe, if I was smart, I'd take last night's purse and put it down as security on an office.

Then again, maybe I wasn't smart. . . .

"You want a job?" Eddie asked me.

"That wasn't what I had in mind, Eddie," I told him. "You're your own man; that's what I—"

Shaking his head, he said, "No, that's not what I meant. Do you want a case, as a referral? Something to work on, keep you busy?"

"Something you don't want to handle?" I asked him.

"Right. I've got a couple of cases that are keeping me busy. I told the client I'd recommend someone. If you want, I'll set up an appointment for you. You can listen to what the man has to say and then decide for yourself if you want it. Fair enough?"

I thought it over, then agreed. Hell, I had the license now, I might as well make some use of it. The extra cash would come in handy. That was no million-dollar purse I'd fought for last night.

"Okay," he said, rubbing his hands together with satisfaction. "Call me later, and I'll let you know if I was able to set it up."

My first case. Suddenly, I wasn't so depressed.

"Okay, Eddie, okay," I told him. "Thanks."

"Forget it, kid. Just remember everything I taught ya—and throw a case my way every once in a while, will ya?"

"You got it. I'll talk to you later, Eddie."

"S'long, kid."

On the way out I gave Missy a cheery good-bye and she graced me with a beautiful smile.

Maybe I should just forget the whole thing and become a florist?

CHAPTER THREE

I found my brother just where I thought I would, in a bar called Packy's, in Greenwich Village.

"Did I find you before you had time to drink up the whole purse?" I asked him.

Benny was five years older than me. He had pushed me into the fight game and appointed himself my manager when his career ended with a vicious knockout that left him with occasional double vision. He was pretty good with the booze while I was training, but I had to watch him the day after a fight to make sure I got my share of the purse before he drank it up.

"Aw, Miles. I got it right here," he told me, and handed me my share. Benny took twenty percent, which left me with eight hundred bucks, my biggest payday to date. Better paydays were coming, he always told me. Yeah, sure, I always told him.

What could I do? He was my brother.

"Look, Benny," I said, showing him my P.I. license.

"You got it, kid," he replied unhappily. Although he knew it was something I had been wanting for a long time, he had always felt that my working for Eddie Waters would interfere with my fighting. My getting my own ticket was an even bigger threat. "Congrats. C'mon, I'll buy you a drink."

"Ginger ale."

He shook his head and muttered, "Athletes. Packy, give the champ a ginger ale."

He turned to the bar and slumped over his drink. I didn't want to get into another argument with him over my license, so I sat next to him and kept my mouth shut.

Packy set my soda down in front of me and said, "I saw the fight last night, Jack. What took you so long to figure the guy out?"

"Well, Packy, I would've had the guy figured out sooner, but he kept hitting me."

Packy was a big, florid-faced man in his early fifties who had known me and Benny since we were kids. He was an ex-heavyweight and still told stories about the time he had gone eight with Marciano, before Marciano was champ. "I coulda beat him," he always said, "if I'da had a crowbar."

He usually charged us half price for drinks when things were slow, and didn't charge us at all when things were going good.

This time he took my dollar and brought back change.

I left it on the bar.

"I just wish for once the ring announcer would get my name right," I added. "Just once I'd like to hear him say *Jack*abee instead of Ja*co*bee."

"When you're champ," Benny told me, "they'll get your friggin' name right."

"Speaking of figuring the guy out, Benny, who was the guy?"

Without turning his head he answered, "What guy?" absently.

"The guy in the fifth row last night, remember?"

He thought it over a moment, then remembered. "Oh, that guy. I don't know, just some guy. Did you a lot of good, didn't he?"

"Yeah, he did that. I'd kind of like to know who he was, though. Did you talk to him yourself?"

"No, he sent me a message with Lucas. 'Count, right-left'—that was the message."

"Lucas, huh?"

Lucas Pratt was a junkie who hung around the Times Square Gym, where I worked out. When I was flush—which was rare—I'd throw him a few bucks. He ran some numbers, other times just delivered messages for walking-around money.

Like last night.

"Maybe Lucas knows," Benny offered. He waved to Packy for another drink.

"Take it easy, okay, Benny?" I said, and gave Packy the eye. Benny smiled and nodded, like he always did, and he'd probably go ahead and get stiff, like he always did.

"Packy, a short leash, huh?" I said aloud. He nodded, but you couldn't stop Benny from getting a drink if he wanted one. At least at Packy's he was among friends.

"I'll see you later, Ben," I told him, climbing down off my stool. I wanted to go and find Lucas Pratt. I was interested in who my mysterious benefactor was from the night before. I owed him a hearty thank you.

I grabbed the subway to Times Square and made my first stop the gym.

"Willy, you seen Lucas today?" I asked one of the trainers.

Without taking his eyes from the boy in the ring, he told me, "Not today, Jack." Then he did look at me and added, "Hey, Jack, you took too long figuring that guy out last night, much too long."

"But I did, didn't I?" I pointed out.

He shook his head. "Don't fight no more southpaws until you get more experience, Jack. And dump Benny. He ain't doing you no good."

"Easy, Willy."

"Hell, boy, I'm telling you for your own good. Keep your brother around if you want, but get yourself a decent manager and a decent trainer."

Willy Wells was about fifty-five or so, a little bantamweight of a man who'd managed some top contenders in his time. He had thinning, sandy-colored hair and a pair of thick glasses on his nose, and he had never gotten along with Benny. Benny had wanted Willy to train him some years back, but Willy had come right out and told Benny that he didn't have what it took and he couldn't afford to spend the time on him. Benny never forgave him for that, especially since he had turned out to be right.

"Like you, Willy?"

"I don't think so, kid. You got too much of your brother in you, but there's a few guys around that I know are interested in you."

"I'll see you around, Willy," I told him, and walked away. He went back to watching his boy in the ring, shouting out instructions.

I asked around some more and went and checked the locker room to see if Lucas was sweeping up. He wasn't around. When I came out of the locker room I saw Willy talking to two guys, pointing in my direction. The two guys were wearing suits and you could smell cop all over them, even from across the room. They started walking toward me, and I waited.

"You Miles Jacoby?" the older one asked. He pronounced it the same way the ring announcer had pronounced it the night before. He had a salt-and-pepper crew cut, which looked funny in this day and age. His face was a mass of wrinkles with a cigar sticking out of one of them. I assumed it was his mouth. The other guy was about ten years younger, maybe thirty-five, taller and lighter.

"I am. What can I do for you?" I answered.

"My name's Detective Hocus. This is my partner, Detective Wright. Understand you're looking for Lucas Pratt?"

"That's right, I am. Is he in some kind of trouble?"

"You could say that; he's dead."

"Dead," I repeated, and it took a moment to sink in. "Dead? What the hell happened? Did he OD?"

"Maybe. Why do you ask that?"

"It's no big secret that Lucas is a junkie," I told them. "What do you mean by 'maybe'?"

"It means, maybe, maybe not. He was found in an arcade on Thirty-Fourth Street. He had a needle sticking out of him, but the coroner said he died before the stuff could go completely through his system. There were traces of stuff, but not enough to kill him. The M.E. says it was possible, but not probable."

"Then what's probable?"

"It's highly probable that he died as a result of his injuries."

I felt like I was being led by the nose, but I asked, "What injuries?"

"Somebody worked him over real good, somebody who was good with his fists." He looked me over deliberately and before I could reply added, "From the looks of you, that description doesn't necessarily apply."

I kept my cool.

"Somebody beat him to death, so naturally you come down here looking for a likely suspect. I think you're barking up the wrong tree, Detective. Lucas was a regular here, he never got in anyone's way. Look somewhere else for your murderer, that's my advice."

"Oh, that's your advice, is it? You a detective as well as a, uh, fighter?" he asked.

"As a matter of fact," I said, taking out my license and showing it to him, "I am."

"Well, well, a private eye," he remarked to his partner, then checking the date of issue added, "and spanking brand-new, too. Well, Mr. Jacoby, I hope you can detect better than you can fight." He handed the license back and said, "We'll be in touch—in case we need any more advice, that is."

I watched them as they walked out and then went over to Willy and said, "Thanks, Willy."

"For what? They asked for somebody who knew Lucas. You just asked me about him, so I told him to talk to you. At .least now you know where Lucas is, right? He's at the morgue."

"Yeah, the morgue. I wonder who made the I.D.?" I mused.

"Who knows? Everybody knew him. He had no family, so one I.D. was good as the next, I guess." He turned away and cursed at his fighter for taking a left from his sparring partner. "You do that in a fight and you're gonna hit the canvas, sucker!"

I walked away without saying anything.

I was sorry Lucas was dead. He had been harmless, but he was also my link to the guy I was looking for. Now my link was gone.

I headed back to Packy's, hoping I would get to Benny before he fell off his stool.

CHAPTER FOUR

When I got back to Packy's, Benny was gone.

"Packy, where'd my brother go?"

Packy shrugged. "You got me, Jack. He left about ten minutes after you did."

"He didn't say where he was going?"

"Not a word, but he was negotiating pretty good."

"Thanks."

I left the bar and decided to check on the unlikely possibility that Benny had gone home. That meant seeing Julie, which I didn't mind at all.

Julie Wilson had married my brother five years ago as his ring career was coming to an end. Why, I'll never know. Julie was a genuine beauty, and my brother was, at best, the proverbial beast, but she married him, and that was that. I love my brother, don't get me wrong; but the catch of the year he ain't, so I really couldn't understand it. Besides that, Julie had always turned me on, and still did. If I'd been around when she met Benny, it might have been different. . . .

They had an apartment in a rundown building on Jane Street, a lot less than Julie deserved.

I had a key to Benny's place, but when I used it once before the results had been somewhat embarrassing. Seems Julie had just finished taking a shower when I walked in. She had been naked, the one and only time I'd ever seen her that way. She was a tall brunette, big-breasted and slim-hipped. She had nipples like cherries, and I had stared at them and the black bush between her legs while we were both frozen with surprise. She was the first to recover and had turned around, walked into her bedroom and put on a silk robe. Neither one of us ever mentioned the incident to Benny or to each other thereafter, but I hadn't used the key since.

I knocked on the door and waited for her to answer. When she did I got that choked-up feeling I always got when I saw her face. It wasn't a classically beautiful face, but still it grabbed me by the throat whenever I saw her. She had dark eyes and a sensuous mouth. Her nose was a little too big, but then again it was perfect for her.

"Miles, hi," she greeted, backing up to allow me to enter. She showed concern over my eye, touching it lightly. I could swear it tingled where she touched it, but it had to be my imagination.

"Congratulations on winning," she told me. "Ben told me it was a knockout."

"Thanks, Julie." She hated fighting, but always congratulated me when I won. "Is he here?"

She looked surprised.

"No, he hasn't come home since he left this morning. I assumed he went to Packy's," she added in a helpless sort of voice. She didn't approve of Ben's drinking habits, but her opinion didn't make a hell of an impact on him. I knew she wasn't happy, yet she stayed with him.

"He was there, but he's not now."

"Was he drunk?"

"I don't think so. He was okay when I left him, and Packy says he left ten minutes after I did. He couldn't have been too bad."

She shrugged and asked, "Can I get you some coffee?"

I would have liked to have a cup of coffee with her, but being alone in the apartment with her made me nervous as hell. I turned it down.

"I've got a few things to do, Julie. I got my license, by the way."

"Oh, I'm so glad for you," she told me, giving me a little hug. "I know you wanted it so badly."

"Thanks," I said, backing away from her a bit. The hug had unnerved me. I got pissed at myself for feeling like a schoolboy who had just been hugged by a teacher he has a crush on. True, she was about four years older than me, but it was far from a teacher-student gap.

She seemed puzzled by my reaction, and I wanted to get out of there before she questioned it.

"I'll see you soon, Julie," I told her.

"Come over for dinner tonight?" she asked.

"Sure."

"A victory dinner," she added. "We'll have a double celebration."

I smiled at her and said, "Okay, thanks. I'll see you tonight."

"I'll tell Ben you're coming."

"Yeah, you do that."

"Miles?"

"Yeah?" I said, with my hand on the knob.

"Now that you've got your license, does that mean that you'll stop fighting?" she asked.

I hesitated, then replied, "It means I'll think about it."

"I guess that's good enough," she said. "See you later."

I left, feeling heady, as I always did after seeing her.

It's a bitch-and-a-half being in love with your brother's wife.

CHAPTER FIVE

I went to the bank next and deposited seven hundred bucks of my winning purse. That gave me three grand in the bank, the results of three years of saving. Isn't that depressing? A grand a year.

Shit.

I hopped a train uptown, got off at Fifty-first and Lexington. I went into an office building across from the subway and rode the elevator to the fifteenth floor. I went to a door marked GALLAGHEN ENTERPRISES and entered.

Dick Gallaghen was a fight promotor, hustler and low-rung Mafia member. He had promoted the card I'd fought on the night before. My fight had been a prelim. The main event had been a bout between two up-and-coming light-heavies, both undefeated. They stayed that way when the judges called the ten-round bout a draw.

It was a good setup for a return match, which would be promoted by Gallaghen, no doubt. Kind of made you think, sometimes.

His secretary, a lovely, light-skinned black girl named Patrice looked up as I entered.

"Hail the conquering—and battered—hero," she sang out.

I gave her my "I ain't pretty but I gets the job done" line.

"You're half right," she agreed.

I didn't ask which half.

"Is he in?"

"Yes, but he's on the phone."

"I'll wait."

As I said that we both noticed the light on her phone go off.

"He's off," she said, and picked up the phone. "Miles Jacoby is here, Mr. Gallaghen. Yes, sir." She hung up and told me, "You can go in, Jack."

"Thanks."

I knocked once and entered.

"Jack, my boy," Gallaghen greeted me. He rose from behind his desk, something that didn't come easy to a man who weighed two fifty or better and was only five six. The ever present Turkish cigarette was burning in the ashtray, with about twenty dead comrades. He smoked at least three packs a day. He's the primest candidate for a heart attack I've ever known, and he's always as healthy as an ox.

I shook his pudgy hand, aware as I always was of the strength that was behind it. He dropped himself back into his chair, grabbed the burning cigarette and sucked it to death. He dropped the butt into the tray and lit another one with a gold lighter, then he invited me to sit.

"Didn't you get your share, or did your brother drink it up?" he asked. Gallaghen was well aware of my brother's failings. In fact, he felt that they were all that my brother had.

"I got it, Dick. I wanted to talk to you about something else," I told him.

"Congratulations on another victory. Not pretty, you know, but you got the job done. I can always count on at least one good fight when I book you, Jack."

"I appreciate that, Dick. Listen, there was somebody at the fight that I want to locate."

"Oh? What's his name?"

"I don't know that. All I know is that he was sitting in the fifth row."

"A guy? Not a broad?"

"It wasn't a broad, it was a guy. He sent Benny a message through Lucas Pratt."

"I heard about Lucas," he told me. "It had to happen sooner or later, I guess."

"I guess."

"What was the message?"

"That's not important. I'd just like to find the guy and talk to him."

Shrugging his shoulders, he asked, "What do you want me to do? Can you describe him?"

"No, I can't. What I want you to do is give me a list of every ticket holder in the fifth row."

He knew I didn't mean "every" ticket holder, because that was impossible. I meant every ticket holder who was somebody. This guy I was after was not just some guy out for a Tuesday night of boxing. The guy knew his stuff, which meant he had to be a pro, a somebody.

"Okay, Jack, I don't see why not. Check with me tomorrow; I'll have Patrice work it up."

"Thanks, Dick. I appreciate it."

"No problem, Kid. What do we have next for you?"

"I've got a bout in two months with Johnny Ricardi," I told him.

"That should give the eye time to heal. Ricardi's a rough boy. Benny set that up?"

"Yes."

"You ready for him?"

"I'm ready."

He shook his head.

"A decent trainer and manager could do wonders for you, Kid, you know that?"

"So I've been told. I didn't come here to discuss my brother, Dick."

"Hey, Kid, hey, I like your brother, I really do. Look, call me tomorrow for that list, okay? You don't mind if I don't get up, right?"

"Thanks, Dick."

I left him looking thoughtful at his desk. As I entered the outer office I saw the light on Patrice's phone go on.

"Hey, how about some dinner after I heal?" I asked her, even though I knew she didn't date fighters.

She looked at me, eyeing me critically.

"That might be a while," she remarked.

"I'm a fast healer," I told her.

"I've heard that before. I really don't see how you men can get into a ring and pound on each other until you bleed," she told me.

"Hey, women are doing it too now. Besides, there are drawbacks to every profession, Pat."

"Don't I know it. I thought working here would give me

an opportunity to meet some eligible athletes, but all I seem to meet are fighters."

"Thanks."

"You're nice, Jack. I could go for you, but you're still a fighter."

"You like florists?" I asked her.

"What?" she asked, puzzled.

"Never mind. I'll see you."

The light on her phone was still on when I left.

CHAPTER SIX

I checked all of Benny's usual hangouts but couldn't locate him anywhere. In fact, no one had seen him all day. I went back to Packy's, but he hadn't been back there either.

He seemed to have disappeared.

Not that I was worried. Benny could take care of himself, as long as he wasn't drunk out of his mind.

Well, maybe I was worried, at that.

I checked another place, a gin mill on Eighth Avenue at Thirty-first Street. He wasn't there, and hadn't been. When I walked out of the joint and realized that I was only a few blocks from where Lucas Pratt's body had been found, I decided to take a look.

The arcade where Lucas had been found was on Thirty-fourth, across the street from Macy's. When I entered I could smell stale urine and fresh pot. The doorway he had been found in was next to a gift shop. I went into the shop and spoke to the old man behind the counter.

"This is where the body was found this morning, isn't it?" I asked him while browsing.

"I don't know nothing," he said in a bored tone.

"You must know that much."

"I don't know nothing," he repeated, with no change in tone.

I took out a five and folded it lengthwise.

"Yeah, so, he was found here," he admitted, eyeing the five.

"By who?"

"By me."

The scent of fresh weed was still in the air.

"You call the cops?"

"'Course. I'm a law abidin' citizen."

"Of course. How'd you find him?"

"Dead."

I stared at him.

"Shit, man, he was just lying there, you know? He had a fuckin' needle stickin' out of his arm, and I knew he was fuckin' dead. I seen dead junkies before, you know? I called the cops, and they came and got him."

I gave him the five and some free advice.

"Tell your customers not to light up as soon as they make their buy. You can smell the stuff a mile away."

"Shit."

"Yeah."

Real detective work, ain't it great? What did that tell me?

I wondered if the arcade was a regular spot for Lucas to shoot up. I guessed only another junkie could tell me that.

I knew a few I could ask.

I hopped a train back to the Village and hunted one up.

The one I found was a guy named Victor Ganetti. I found him in his regular stairwell, coked to the gills. I hoped I'd be able to get something out of him.

"Hey, Vickie, it's me, Miles Jacoby."

"Hey, Jack, buddy," he called back, coming halfway up the stairs. "Heard you won last night, man. Attaway, José." He started to giggle and I waited until he stopped.

"You hear about Lucas, Vickie?"

His sunken cheeks sunk a little more and he nodded sadly, tears coming to his already red eyes.

"Heard, man, heard. Hot shit, hot shot, you know? Tough. Poor, poor, Lucas, man."

"You know where he was found?"

"Yeah, arcade, sure."

"Was that a regular spot for him, Vickie?"

"Spot? Shit, no, man. Him and me, we shoot up together, you know? Down here, man, never uptown."

Thirty-fourth was midtown, but I knew what he meant. They never shot up north of Fourteenth Street.

He started to giggle and blubber at the same time, and I knew I was going to lose him. I took a second five out of my pocket and shoved it into his.

"Be good, Vickie."

"Thanks, man. Too bad 'bout Lucas, man. Hot shit, hot shot, man. Holy shit!"

"Yeah."

I left him and went back to Packy's. Benny still wasn't there.

"Packy, ginger ale."

He brought it over and took my dollar.

When he brought back the change he said, "Hey, your sister-in-law called before, looking for you."

"For me, or for Benny?"

"She didn't even mention Benny, man, just asked for you. Sounded out of breath, too, like she'd just gone a four-round exhibition with Ali."

In spite of myself I started having visions of Julie and me sitting down to dinner without Benny.

"How long ago did she call?"

He shrugged. "Hour, maybe more."

I checked my watch. It was almost five, and she usually had dinner on by six.

I let my ginger ale stand where it was and left.

When she opened the door in answer to my knock, she practically fell into my arms.

"Oh, Miles, thank God."

The way she was dressed she looked like she was ready to go out.

"Julie, what is it? What's wrong?" I asked her, holding her tightly against me. She was shivering.

"I tried to find you, Miles, I tried," she said into my shoulder. "I've been trying to find you for hours."

I held her at arm's length and asked her again, "Honey, what's wrong."

"It's Benny, Miles. He's—he's been arrested!"

Was that all? Benny had gotten drunk and ended up getting himself thrown in the tank before.

"C'mon, Julie. It's not the first time—"

"No, you don't understand," she told me, shaking her head. "He wasn't arrested for being drunk."

"Then what?"

"He—he was arrested for—for murder!"

CHAPTER SEVEN

She had gotten the call from the cops—Detective Hocus, she said—at about two that afternoon. They wanted her to come down to the Seventeenth Precinct. She was afraid to go alone, so she'd been trying to get me ever since then. She said she wouldn't have known what to do down there if she had gone alone. I held her tight, telling her it was all right, until she calmed down, then told her to get her jacket. We went to the precinct together.

I asked for Detective Hocus, and a uniformed officer guided us up some stairs to a room filled with desks and people.

Hocus was standing at the far end and came over when he saw us.

"Mrs. Jacoby?" he asked Julie.

"Y-yes."

"I'm glad you could finally make it," he told her, and I didn't like his tone. "Please, come this way."

He led us to a cubicle and allowed us to precede him in.

"Well, the private eye, huh?" he said to me, remembering who I was. "What's your interest in this?"

"This is my brother-in-law, Officer," Julie told him.

"That's my brother you locked up, Hocus," I added.

He showed surprise.

"I should have made the connection," he said, as if scolding himself. "Sit down, both of you."

27

He closed the door and seated himself behind the desk in the room.

"This office is not mine, it's my lieutenant's," he confided to us, "but he's not in today, so we can use it."

"Great," I told him.

He turned to Julie and asked her, "Are you happily married, Mrs. Jacoby?" He was mispronouncing the name, but neither one of us bothered to correct him.

"What?" Julie asked, thrown off balance by the question.

"I asked you about your marriage, Mrs. Jacoby. Is it a happy one?"

"I—why, yes, but I don't—"

"It took you almost four hours to come down here, ma'am, after I called you and told you that your husband had been arrested—"

"It's not the first time my brother has been arrested, Detective Hocus," I informed him.

"I know that," he told me, and held up a folder to show me why. He had Benny's record right there. "But for murder?" He turned to Julie again and added, "I was just wondering why it took you so long to come down?"

"She didn't want to come down alone—" I started to say, but he cut me off.

"I'd rather she answer the question, if you don't mind?" he asked me.

"Look, I don't see—"

"Would you rather I questioned her alone?" he asked me.

Since the reason I had come with her was so she wouldn't be alone, I shut up. At the same time, Julie touched my arm and said, "It's all right, Miles."

Addressing herself to Hocus she told him, "I didn't want to come down alone, Detective. I was trying to find my brother-in-law to come down with me. I also thought that he should know what was happening."

"Are you and your brother-in-law close?"

"Wait a minute—" I started, unable to see the relevancy of the question.

Julie touched my arm again and said, "Let me, Miles. Yes, Detective, my brother-in-law and I are quite close. In fact, all three of us are close. Do you find something suspicious in that?"

"Not at all. Please, ma'am, don't take offense. I only meant—"

"I know exactly what you meant, and I do take offense. Now, if you don't mind, I'd like to see my husband."

"Of course," he told her. He got up and went out to get a uniformed cop. When he returned with one he told the cop, "Take Mrs. Jacoby down to see her husband."

The young cop, who's nameplate identified him as Nowich, said, "Right. Would you follow me, ma'am?"

I started to get up, and Hocus snapped, "Not you, private eye. Just her."

"He's my brother."

"I want to talk to you."

I sat back down and nodded to Julie. She followed the uniform out.

"Has he called a lawyer?" I asked.

"He really wasn't in shape to do much of anything," he told me.

"Was he drunk?"

"Stewed."

"Look, what's going on? What's this bullshit about my brother killing somebody?"

"That's the charge. Is your brother given to violence?"

"My brother is not a violent man. I'm the fighter in the family, not him. I don't even think he knows how to fight," I told him, and then added to myself: anymore. "Look, what the hell happened?"

"Okay, here's how we got it. He burst into a guy's office today. They started arguing, the guy's secretary got scared, so she called for a radio car. When the car got there the girl was waiting for them on the street. She said she thought your brother had killed her boss. The guys from the car went up with her and found her boss dead. Your brother was found in the building, apparently looking for another way out. Or maybe he was just too drunk to find the front door. Anyway, we got called to the scene and we brought your brother here. He couldn't tell us much in his condition, but we found his phone number on him and called his wife."

"Has he been charged?"

He shook his head.

"He hasn't been booked and formally charged, but he will be. As far as I can see," he added frankly, "he's guilty."

"Is that for you to decide?" I demanded, getting hot.

"He's guilty, what can I tell you?" he asked me. "There was nobody else there."

"Who's he supposed to have killed?" I asked.

"One of you guys."

"What does that mean?"

"I mean he killed a shamus, another private eye."

"Who?"

"A guy named Waters, Eddie Waters."

CHAPTER EIGHT

I've caught a lot of rights and lefts in my time, but that was the hardest punch I'd ever been hit with.

My brother, arrested for killing my best friend.

"That's crazy," I said, surprised at how calmly I'd said it. "That's absolute lunacy, Hocus. Believe me, my brother couldn't kill anybody."

"I'd like to believe you, kid, really I would, but I'm a cop. I'm only allowed to believe what I see, not what people tell me. What I see is the evidence," he said, showing me one finger, "and what the evidence tells me," he went on, showing me the second finger, "is that your brother killed Eddie Waters."

I quelled my first instinct, which was to argue, but how could I argue with evidence? I couldn't, not unless I could find some way to refute it.

After all, I was a detective, wasn't I? At least, that was what my brand-new license said.

"How was he killed?"

"He was beat to death. Shit, he was a bloody mess, kid, all tore up, outside and in. He was beaten by somebody who knew what they were doing."

Like an ex-pug.

I wondered if Hocus knew that Benny had been in the ring and was just waiting to see if I'd mention it.

Well, if he was he'd wait a hell of a long time before I'd say something that would hurt Benny.

Even if he was . . .

"How did your brother and Waters get along?" Hocus asked, and I was grateful he'd broken into my thoughts.

"Uh, fine," I said, and then decided that the best thing to do for Benny would be to not get caught in a lie. Not telling him about Benny's ring career, that was just leaving something out, but telling him that Eddie and Benny got along fine, well, that was just an out-and-out lie.

He was watching me, waiting for me to make up my mind. I made up my mind about Hocus, just then. I figured him for a good cop.

"Okay, so they didn't get along all that well," I admitted.

"Why not?"

"They fought—well—argued over me, mostly. Benny, he wants me to be middleweight champ of the world. Eddie can't—couldn't understand why I'd get in the ring and let people beat on me with their fists. He helped me get my license."

"How did your brother feel about that?"

I shrugged. "He wasn't all that thrilled, I admit, but he wouldn't go to Eddie and—"

"You think Waters's secretary lied?"

No, I didn't think that. Missy wouldn't lie about something that serious.

"No, I don't think she lied. If she says Benny was there, then he was there."

"And if she says your brother killed Eddie Waters?"

"Now wait a minute, Hocus. You said that she told the men who responded that she *thought* my brother was *killing* Eddie Waters. She *thought!*"

"And then they found him dead."

"And that doesn't mean that my brother killed him!" I insisted.

"Well, I'm sorry, kid. I'll present the evidence that I have to the D.A. and I'm sure he'll want to go ahead with an indictment."

"And that's the end of it? No more investigation, huh? You're so damned sure you've got your man?"

He held up his hands and said, "Whoa! I didn't say the investigation was over, but as far as the second part of that statement goes, yes, I do think we have our man."

"Shit!"

"Do you want to see your brother now?"

"Yes."

He went to get a uniform and came back with the same man as before—Nowich.

"Take Mr. Jacoby to see his brother." He turned to me and said, "Listen, private eye, don't be getting any ideas about interfering with a police investigation. My investigation is still progressing. Your brother will get as fair a shake as we can give him."

"Sure," I said, from a man who's already convicted him. What kind of shake was that?

"Keep in touch," Hocus threw at me as I walked out of the room.

I followed the officer and he took me to a room downstairs, where I found Julie and Benny.

When Nowich shut the door behind me the first thing I said was, "Eddie, goddamnit!"

His head had been in his hands, and now he raised his head and looked at me. He looked like shit, worse than he had ever looked at the end of any bender he'd been on.

"Miles, I didn't—I didn't kill him, Miles, I didn't—" he told me, stammering.

"But you did go to his office, right?" I demanded, leaning on the table they were sitting at.

"Miles—" Julie said, but I ignored her.

"Yes, I did."

"What the hell for, Benny?"

"To talk to him, just to talk to him, I swear!"

"You mean to argue with him. About my license, right?"

"Miles, I— Oh, hell, I just didn't like the idea of him helping you get it, is all. I want you to be champ, Miles. You can't be a detective, too." He put his hand in his hands and kept muttering, "I just wanted—wanted to—to talk—"

"Benny, Benny . . . all the talking in the world wasn't going to change the way I felt. You knew that. Why'd you have to go and pick a fight with Eddie—"

"I didn't fight with him!" he shouted.

"Well, you sure as hell did more than talk to him!" I shouted back. "You scared Missy so much she called the cops. Now what went on there?"

"Miles, not now, please," Julie said, putting her hand on my arm.

"Julie, I've got to—"

"Please," she said again, tugging on my arm. "He can't talk now."

"No, he can't talk now, because he's still drunk," I said with disgust. Benny looked at me, then buried his face in his hands again.

"Ah—" I said, and walked to the door and banged on it.

"Miles, where are you going?" Benny called out.

"I'm going to get you a lawyer, Benny, because you sure as hell are going to need one."

CHAPTER NINE

"You're putting me on the spot, Miles," Hector Domingo Gonzales Delgado told me.

"I know it, Heck," I replied.

He began to tap the top of his desk with a pencil, and I waited for him to make up his mind.

I knew a number of lawyers, all of whom I had met while working for Eddie Waters. Heck Delgado was the one I chose to contact about defending Benny. Heck was a young guy—thirty-two or so—who had his own practice and did all right for himself. He was very friendly with Eddie—who had, in fact, helped him get started—and that's what he meant when he told me I was putting him on the spot.

"Do you think your brother killed Eddie, Miles?" he asked.

My first instinct was to say no, but I wanted to play fair with Heck, and I prefaced my answer by telling him just that.

"To be fair with you, Heck, I don't honestly know at this point. I didn't get all that much out of Benny last night, and I can't make up my mind until I've heard his story."

"And Missy's," he pointed out.

"And Missy's," I agreed.

Heck stood up, giving me a good look at his three-piece suit. He was tall and athletically trim, every girl's dream of a handsome, sexy, successful lawyer. He was unmarried, and I knew that he tried very hard to make every girl's dream come true—just short of marriage, that is.

He had a Ricardo Montalban accent that thickened anytime he became agitated or upset, which is why he worked very hard at always maintaining his cool, especially in court.

"I'm giving you an out, Heck. You can say no without affecting our friendship in any way."

"I appreciate that, Miles, I really do, but the fact remains that your brother is entitled to a competent defense. If I said no, I would be worried that he would not get one." He spread his hands and asked me, "Who is more competent than I?"

"No one," I said, giving him the answer he sought. He smiled and stepped forward, extending his hand. I took it and shook it firmly—and gratefully.

"Of course I will defend your brother," he told me, clasping my hand in both of his. "I will speak with him today."

"I'd like to sit in," I told him.

He held a finger up at me and said, "If I am to be your brother's attorney, you must allow me to conduct his defense my way, Miles."

"Of course, but—"

"I will speak to him alone, Miles. I do not want him to be influenced by your presence."

"Will you tell me what he says?"

"Up to a point."

"What do you mean?"

"Your brother must be the one to hire me," he explained. "I'll talk to him today. If he chooses to do so, my only responsibility will be to him. I will tell you anything he agrees to let me tell you. This is the way I work, Miles."

"I understand," I assured him, "but I'm going to be working on this, Heck."

He shook his head, walked around behind his desk and seated himself again. He made a bridge out of his hands and regarded me critically over them.

"I would advise against that, Miles."

"I thought you might."

"You are too emotionally involved with this case, but aside from that, it is a homicide and as such is a police matter. I respect your abilities, I really do, but you have no experience in matters such as this. You might do your brother more harm than good."

I was about to reply, but he held up one hand to stop me.

"Let's not argue the point. Think about it and make your own decision. Will you let your sister-in-law know that I would like to go downtown with her? I prefer to do it that way. She will introduce me to the investigating officer, making it seem as if she was the one to bring me into it."

"I'll let her know right away."

"Tell her I'll pick her up at"—he checked his watch, then said—"ten-thirty this morning." I had come to his office at nine, hoping to catch him before he went to court. If he was going to pick Julie up at ten-thirty, he must not have had any court appearances scheduled for that day.

"Here's the address," I said, writing it on a piece of his stationery. He took it, glanced at it and tucked it away in his breast pocket.

Getting up, I said, "I appreciate this, Heck."

He waved my appreciation away and said, "You might not. Let's wait and see, shall we?"

"I'll go over and tell Julie to expect you. In fact, I might see you there."

"Fine. Miles?"

"Yeah?" I said, stopping at the door.

"I'll do the best I can," he promised.

"I know it, Heck. I'll see you."

CHAPTER TEN

The cops were finished with Eddie's office, so I was able to use my key to let myself in.

I had gone from Hector's office to Julie's apartment, to let her know that Heck would be along to take her downtown.

"What about you?" she asked. "Are you coming?"

"No, Heck doesn't want me around when he interviews Ben," I told her.

"And you don't really want to come anyway, do you?" she asked.

"Julie—"

She held up her hand, then put it on my arm and said, "It's all right, Miles. I understand. Eddie Waters was your friend."

"And Ben is my brother."

She rubbed her hand on my arm, as if to soothe me, but it was having the opposite effect. "You do what you have to do, Miles. I'll understand," she promised.

I backed away from the touch of her hand, hopefully without seeming to.

"I'll do everything I can do to clear Ben, Julie. You know that."

"I know it," she assured me.

"But you're right. I just don't want to see him right now. Tell him—tell him I'm sorry about yesterday, about shouting at him. Tell him—"

"I'll tell him, Miles, don't worry."

As I was leaving she said, "Call me later?"

After that I went straight to Eddie's office. It was locked, but the police seal on the door had been broken, indicating that they had gotten all the evidence they were going to get from within. I unlocked the door and walked in.

I stood just inside the doorway, listening to the silence. I'd never been in the office when it wasn't inhabited by either Missy or Eddie himself. It was an odd feeling. I felt like I was in Eddie's tomb.

I walked through the anteroom to Eddie's office and sat down in front of his desk. I imagined him sitting behind his desk, as he had been so many times, teaching me, scolding me, encouraging me.

Now he was dead, and if Benny didn't kill him, who did?

I got up and walked to Eddie's file cabinets. The answer just might be in one of these drawers, I told myself, but which one? It could take me forever to sort them out, open cases from closed cases, most likely and least likely. I had never been involved with the files. That was Missy's responsibility, and she was the only one who could help me and save me a hell of a lot of time.

If she would do it.

Missy had been very close to Eddie, not as a lover, but as a friend. He had given her a job when she was alone in the city, had given her something to take her mind off being alone. She had worked for him for eight years. If she was convinced that Ben had killed him, would she help me try to prove otherwise?

There was only one way for me to find that out.

I left the building and walked to Fifty-third and Third, where I caught the downtown train. At Delancey Street I changed to the M train to Queens. Missy had a house in Middle Village, and I was some detective because there I was on the train already and I hadn't even called to make sure she was home. One of Eddie's primary rules of private detecting was, "When you're on a case, *never* waste time." A ride to Missy's house when she wasn't even there sure came under the heading of wasting time.

It was a good thing I lucked out.

She was home.

I walked to her house from the subway and rang the bell. I was about to hit it again when she opened the door. She'd been crying, and recently.

40

"Hello, Missy."

"Jack," she said, and started crying again. "Come on in," she said through the tears.

I'd never been to her house before. It was well kept, and from where I was I could see the living room and the dining room. Also a stairway leading upstairs.

Missy was wearing a bathrobe, and her hair wasn't combed, but she still looked fine to me. The robe was a short, terry-cloth type and showed off her legs and thighs, a fact she seemed totally unaware of. I couldn't say the same for me.

"Missy," I began, sitting next to her. "I need your help."

"I was just on the phone with the police," she said, as if she hadn't heard me. "They told me that I could go ahead and make funeral arrangements, they'd be releasing the body in a few days."

"You're taking care of the arrangements?" I asked her.

She nodded, holding a handkerchief to her nose. "Eddie didn't have any family."

That stopped me because I never knew that about Eddie, and I felt that I should have. I guess there were a lot of things I didn't know about him.

"He was my friend," I said out loud, "I should have known that."

She looked at me and then touched my face with her hand.

"He used to say that you and I were the only family he had, Jack," she told me, then fell against me and started crying again. I held her until she was all cried out, and then she offered to make some coffee. I agreed, only because it would give her something to do and a chance to pull herself together.

By the time she came back with two cups of coffee, she seemed to have control of herself.

"Thanks, Missy."

She made a face and said, "I hate that name. Eddie was the only one to call me that, until I met you, then you started."

"I only called you that because he did," I said in my defense.

"I know, I know. I tried to break him of the habit, but I finally gave up." She sipped her coffee, staring straight ahead. I knew she was looking at something that I couldn't see, so I tried to keep the conversation alive so she wouldn't have the time to start crying again.

"What's your real name?"

She made another face and said, "I hate that one, too. Just call me Missy," she told me, "it's the lesser of the two evils."

"Missy"—she made a face again, but I went on—"I need your help."

"To do what?" she asked.

I hesitated a moment, because I knew my next remark was going to remind her that I was Ben's brother.

"I have to clear Ben, Missy." I finally said.

"Oh, no," she said, putting down her cup and getting up from the couch. She took a few steps toward the middle of the room with her arms crossed in front of her.

"Missy—"

She turned quickly and said, "Jack, I know he's your brother, I know that, but he killed Eddie!"

"Honey," I said, getting up and taking her by the shoulders, "did you see Ben do it?"

"No, I didn't *see* him, but—"

"Missy, I don't think my brother is a killer, but since I didn't see what happened, I can't be that sure. Can you?"

She said, "I—" a couple of times and then I went on.

"I have to find out for sure, honey, for myself, and I need your help. Whether Benny did it or not, I have to know for sure. Missy, I need your help to go through Eddie's files."

"The files? What for?"

"If Ben didn't do it, somebody else must have. It has to have something to do with one of Eddie's cases. It would take me forever to go through those files myself," I explained. "I need you to pull out the recent ones so I can go over them. I also need you to tell me if Eddie has had any, uh, disagreements recently with any of his clients, that sort of thing. Missy, I think we owe it to Eddie to make sure the right man is punished for killing him."

She digested that a moment, rubbing her arms as if she felt a chill, then said, "And I guess you owe it to your brother, too, huh?"

"I owe it to myself to find out if my brother really did kill my best friend," I replied.

We stared at each other for a few moments, and then she said, "Give me some time to shower and change."

"I'll get a cab."

"There's a car service number by the phone," she said from the steps. "Tell them half an hour."

"Okay."

I told them half an hour; they were there in forty minutes; she was ready in fifty. There wasn't much conversation during the ride. I was wondering how Heck was doing with Benny. I had no way of knowing what was going on in Missy's head, but I could imagine. She was probably wondering if she was doing the right thing in helping me. I hoped, for her sake, that it would turn out that she was.

When we got to the office I used my key to open the door, but she balked at going in.

"Missy—"

"Just give me a minute, Jack," she told me, holding up one hand, "just a minute, okay?"

"Okay."

"Go on in. I'll be along," she assured me.

I went in ahead of her, through the anteroom into Eddie's office. I was puzzled by her reactions and wondered if I had been wrong in assuming that she and Eddie had never been more than friends.

I went into his office and automatically headed for the visitor's chair before catching myself. I hesitated to sit at his desk, but that was plain silly. It wasn't his desk anymore, because he was gone. I sat down in his chair and waited for Missy to come in. When she did she started a bit when she saw me sitting behind the desk but recovered and sat in the visitor's chair.

"I guess if that desk does belong to anyone now it's you," she said.

I wasn't sure how to take the remark.

"You want to switch places?" I asked her.

"No," she said, shaking her head, "and I'm sorry, Jack. I didn't mean to sound like—"

"Missy, forget it."

She looked down at the floor, and I thought she was going to start crying again. I got up and walked around the desk and crouched down next to her.

"Honey, were you and Eddie..." I started and let it trail off. She knew what I meant though, because she put her hand to her mouth, started crying and nodded her head.

"I'm sorry," I told her, letting her put her head on my shoulder. "I didn't know."

She struggled to regain her composure, succeeded and said, "Nobody knew, Jack, nobody."

"Okay, honey, it's okay," I said, repeating those stupid words that everyone says when they know it damn well isn't "okay."

"I'm sorry, Jack," she said, finally, sitting up straight. "We came here to do something, so let's do it."

"Missy, if I leave you alone here to pull the files, will you be all right?" I asked her.

"Leave? Why?"

"I have to see Hector about my brother."

"Hector Delgado?"

I nodded. "I've asked Heck to defend Ben—or, at least, to talk to him. It's the results of that talk I'm interested in. I'd just be in the way here, anyway. I can't get started until you've pulled the files."

"I guess you're right," she agreed. "What files do you want pulled?"

"I want his most recent cases going, oh, two or three months back, I guess. Make a notation on the ones he might have had problems with. You know, dissatisfied customer, difficult client, anything you think I should know about."

She nodded as I spoke, and then she added, "I'll just pile them up on the desk for you. If you're not back by about six, I'll go on home . . . and yes, I'll be fine, Jack, don't worry."

"I know you will," I told her. I kissed her on the cheek and headed for the door.

"Jack?"

"Yeh?"

She was turned around in her chair, and her face was serious as she told me, "I still think your brother did it . . . but I'm willing to be convinced otherwise."

"I appreciate that, Missy, and I love you for it. I'll call you later tonight."

She smiled wanly and nodded. I smiled back and waved. She was okay, that girl. She could've said the hell with my brother and the hell with me, but she'd been around Eddie too long—and been close to him too long—to do that.

Besides, weren't we part of the same family?

CHAPTER ELEVEN

"That story sounds kind of flaky," I admitted.

"I'm glad you were the one to say it, Miles," Heck told me.

"You mean, neither one of you believes him?" Julie asked us.

I left it to Hector to explain.

"That's not really the point, Mrs. Jacoby," he told her. "If his story sounds funny to us—whether we believe him or not—can you imagine how it must sound to the police?"

"I see your point," she told him.

We were at Julie's apartment, discussing Heck's interview with Benny. My brother's story was an unoriginal one: he remembered drinking, going to see Eddie, and getting into an argument, but beyond that things got kind of hazy. In fact, beyond that, things disappeared altogether.

According to Benny.

Did I believe him?

Hell, I wanted to . . . but ask me again later.

Benny claimed he didn't even remember being taken into custody. The arresting officer had stated that he was definitely out of it when they grabbed him.

"Has Ben ever had blackout before?" Heck asked. "Alcohol-induced or otherwise?"

"Just the normal morning-after blank spaces, but nothing this complete that I know of," I answered, looking at Julie.

"No," she told Heck, "nothing like this."

"What do you say, Heck?" I asked him. "Will you defend Ben?"

He put down the coffee cup he was drinking from and looked at both of us.

"I believe your brother was honest with me, Miles," he said, looking directly at me, "as far as his feelings for Eddie Waters went. He didn't like Waters, and he felt that he was hurting your boxing career. That gives him a definite motive, but he was honest with me about it. If Mrs. Jacoby wants me to, I would like to handle his case."

He looked at Julie, who in turn looked at me. I nodded, and she said, "Thank you, Mr. Delgado."

"*Por nada*," he said, then added, "yet."

"Would you like some more coffee?" Julie asked him.

"I'm afraid I have some other business matters to attend to," he told her, standing up. I could see that he was affected by her, as most men were, and it brought out the charm in him all the more. He took her hand and told her, "I will do the very best that I can for your husband, Mrs. Jacoby."

"If that's the case, Mr. Delgado, then I insist that you call me Julie," she told him, gracing him with a smile.

"Very well . . . Julie," he agreed. I thought for a moment that he would kiss her hand, but he gave it a little shake, then extended it to me for a much firmer one.

"Thanks, Heck."

"You insist on thanking me before I have done anything," he told me. "*Bien*, then you are welcome. Miles, call me tomorrow, eh? There are things we must discuss."

I frowned, but said, "All right, Heck. I'll call you."

He nodded, said good night to Julie again, and I showed him to the door. When I returned to the small living room, Julie had her hands up in front of her mouth, and for a moment I thought she was crying. When she dropped her hands, I saw that she was laughing.

"What's funny?" I asked her.

"He is."

"Why?"

"I don't know," she said, groping for the right words, "but he's so . . . so . . ."

"Ricardo Montalbanish?"

"That's it, exactly," she exclaimed, pressing her hands together and pointing at me with the two index fingers.

"Yeah, I've always thought that," I told her, and then we

were both laughing. Suddenly, the smile faded from her face and she sobered.

"Now what?" I asked.

"It's not right," she said. "Benny's in jail and here I am laughing."

She hugged her arms, as if she were suddenly chilled. I stepped close to her and took her by the elbows.

"Don't feel guilty about laughing, Julie," I told her.

She looked me straight in the eyes and said, "I don't think it's the laughter I feel guilty about, Miles." She put her hands on my chest and I started to pull her toward me, but stopped.

We were both thinking the same thing, but she was the first to put it into words.

"Miles, I think you'd better go. I—I'm a little tired, you know? It's been a long..."

"I know."

"...day, and..."

"I'll call you tomorrow, Julie," I said as she trailed off. I let go of her elbows and backed away, then turned and headed for the door before something happened that we'd both regret later.

Down on the street I knew I didn't want to go home and be alone tonight, so I did something I had sworn I'd never do again.

I went to Tracy's.

CHAPTER TWELVE

"Not bad for a substitute, huh?" Tracy asked.

"Pipe down, will you?" I told her irritably.

Tracy Dean was a substitute and she knew it. On top of that, she didn't mind. Not as long as we both admitted it out front, she had told me long ago. Still, afterward I always felt bad, guilty. It wasn't fair to Tracy. Not that we didn't have a genuine affection for each other, because we did. Our arrangement would never have worked without that. I simply felt guilty because *that* wasn't the only reason I went to her.

Tracy couldn't have given a shit less what my real reasons were. She just enjoyed sex, and she enjoyed having sex with me. She was an energetic little brunette of about twenty-four with round little tits, a perfectly shaped little ass, and a little-girl face, all of which served her well in her chosen fields of endeavor. She was a model and an actress, although the only epics she'd starred in to date were a shade on the blue side, and the only modeling she'd done was her hands, for gloves.

Still, she had a lot of ambition, and a lot of patience to go with it.

We'd met because she was a fight fan and had attended a title fight at the garden for which I had fought a bout on the undercard. She had come to my dressing room afterward to introduce herself, and we just took it from there. On a subsequent night, I got a little too drunk, and it wasn't very hard

49

for her to figure out from things I'd said what my feelings for my sister-in-law were.

So that's where we stood. We were friends and occasional lovers, with no illusions about why we slept together.

"Must have been a rough one tonight," she observed from my mood.

I looked over at her on her side of *her* bed and said, "I'm sorry, I didn't mean to snap at you."

"Oh, that's okay. It comes with the territory," she assured me. "You want a drink, or some coffee?"

"Coffee."

"'Kay."

She bounced off the bed and into the little kitchenette of her tiny Christopher Street apartment.

"Was it?" she called out.

"Was it what?" I asked.

"Rough."

I thought back to that moment when Julie and I were alone in her apartment with absolutely no danger of being discovered by Benny or anyone.

"Yeah, it was a rough one," I told her.

"I'm sorry, Jack," she said, and she genuinely was. Tracy liked for her friends to be happy, and when they weren't, she was sorry.

"Forget it."

"How's Benny? I heard about what happened."

"Benny's okay," I assured her. "I got him a good lawyer, and he's going to be okay." I hoped.

"That's good. I was real sorry to hear about Eddie Waters, but I didn't for a minute believe that Benny killed him."

"Benny'll appreciate that."

She brought two cups of coffee to the bed, handed me one and sat Indian fashion on the bed with the other one.

"You gonna play the great detective now?" she asked.

"What do you mean?"

"You know what I mean, Jack. You've wanted to be Lew Archer for a long time, and now's your chance. This has all the drama you'd ever want because you're personally involved."

I was about to retort, but she didn't give me a chance.

"Don't yell at me," she told me, raising one hand like a traffic cop. "Think about it. I'm an actress, remember? I know what a sense of the dramatic you have."

Leave it to little Tracy to lay it all on the table. Okay, so okay, damnit, the whole situation did appeal to my sense of the dramatic, and although I saw myself as more of a middleweight Mike Hammer, she was right about that, too.

"You're right."

"I know I'm right, but that doesn't mean you have to feel guilty about it. If you didn't have that sense of the dramatic, you might just sit tight and do nothing. You'd never forgive yourself for that if Benny didn't get off."

I sipped the coffee—she made the worst coffee I'd ever tasted—and said, "What makes you so smart, little girl?"

"Hey," she said, frowning, "it's the girls with *big* tits that have small brains, remember?"

I put my coffee cup down and reached out to fondle her left breast. It was small, but round and firm, with large, penny-brown areola and nipple.

"They may not be big—" I began, but she rolled her eyes upward and said, "Please, God, get me a man who'll love me for my mind."

I pinched her nipple, and she squealed and almost scalded us both with her coffee.

I jumped off the bed and started to get dressed.

"Where you going?" she demanded.

"You said it yourself," I warned her. "I'm going out to play detective."

I got one leg into my pants, then started doing a dance trying to get the other one in and ended up falling on my ass. She peered down at me from the bed and said in her worst Bogie imitation, "What's the matter, shamus, get off on the wrong foot?"

CHAPTER THIRTEEN

Knock Wood Lee made book for a living, but he ran some girls on the side for extra cash. I placed my out-of-town bets with him, and he always paid off promptly when he lost. He also seemed to have his fingers into almost everything that went on south of Times Square. If you needed information, and it wasn't going to hurt him personally, he'd give it to you—sometimes for a price, sometimes for a favor, and sometimes for nothing. You could never tell with Wood.

Wood's bottom lady was a China doll named Tiger Lee. She had long, black hair parted down the center and a nice little body with more tits than you'd usually find on a Chinese girl.

When I knocked on the door of Wood's Chelsea loft, it was Lee who answered.

"Welcome, Mr. Jacoby," she greeted me in heavily accented English. That was her "John" voice. Lee was born and raised in Brooklyn and at best had limited command of the Chinese language; but she had learned long ago that the "Johns" loved that singsong Oriental accent when they were in the sack with a Chinese girl, so she used it. She could turn it on and off, like a faucet.

Her days of hooking for a living were over, however, and at the ripe old age of twenty-six she had become Knock Wood Lee's lady.

In spite of the presence of the name *Lee* in both of their

names, they were not related by marriage or in any other way. I called her Lee, and him Wood, to avoid confusion, and I suspect others did the same.

"Is Wood here, Lee?" I asked her.

"Inside. You are welcome, as always." She bowed, and I returned the bow, then she said, "Jesus, I wish we'd seen your face before we paid off. You sure you won that fight?"

I touched my stitches and said, "That's what they tell me. I don't remember a thing after the first punch."

"Yours or his?" she asked, and took me to see Wood.

Wood's businesses—book, girls, games, whatever—were all conducted elsewhere. This was his home, and he took the concept of home as a man's castle very seriously.

Wood jumped up out of his chair when he saw me, hand extended.

"Ah, my good friend, how are you?" he asked.

Wood was only twenty-four, about an inch taller than Tiger Lee's five three. He held a black belt in both karate and judo, however, so his size—or lack of same—was hardly a liability. By the time he was twenty he was a successful bookie in Chinatown, where he was born, and since then he had expanded his horizons. He had longish, black hair and a quick, infectious smile.

He was also extremely dangerous when crossed.

"Beer?" he asked as we sat.

"Sure."

"Lee?"

"I'll get it," she said, and went off to do just that.

Wood's real name was Nok Woo Lee, but that just sort of automatically translated into Knock Wood. Rumor had it that Tiger Lee's real name was Anna Lee, but nobody knew for sure.

Lee came back with three ice-cold Beck's and passed them out. She took a ladylike pull from her own bottle and sat down on the arm of Wood's big, leather chair.

"Sorry I missed your fight," Wood told me. "I heard you won, but to look at you—"

"I think I'm getting tired of hearing that," I told him, surprised at myself because I really was getting annoyed at all the remarks concerning the condition of my face.

Wood put up one hand and said, "Oops, excuse me, sorry. Is this a social visit?"

"No," I answered, and took a long pull on my beer. "Have you heard about Eddie Waters?"

"I saw something in the papers," he answered, and I realized that I hadn't seen a newspaper that day. I made a mental note to pick one up when I left Wood's.

As far as Wood's reaction to the death of Eddie Waters, it was just about what I expected. Wood and Eddie had never been the best of friends.

"I am more distressed by the fact that they have arrested your brother for murder," he said honestly.

"Well, I appreciate that."

"Have you engaged an attorney for him?"

"I have—or rather, his wife has. I recommended Hector Delgado."

He nodded, saying, "Good choice. He's an excellent man." He disposed of half of his beer and asked, "If you have that caliber of man working for you, what is it you want of me?"

"I need a different kind of help from you, Wood. I'd like you to tell me if you know anything about a contract being put out on Eddie Waters."

"A contract? You think it was a professional hit?" he asked.

"I don't know, Wood. I'm asking."

He drank the remainder of the beer and passed the empty to Lee. She still had half of hers left. I had about a third left and swirled it in the bottle while I waited for Wood to answer.

Wood leaned forward and asked, "Did you get your license, Jack?"

"I got it."

"You gonna work on this?"

"I intend to."

Shaking his head, he told me, "Murder is police business, you know?"

"So I've been told, but Ben is my brother."

He looked at me a moment, then leaned back in his chair and said, "I haven't heard anything about a contract having been put out on Eddie Waters. As far as I'm concerned, he was far too small-time for anybody to bother."

I let the remark pass.

"Wood, have you heard anything that might give me a lead?" I asked.

"Nothing."

I waited for more, but that was all that was forthcoming, so I asked, "Will you let me know if you do?"

This was one of the times, if you watched closely, you realized that Tiger Lee was around for much more than just decorative purposes, or fetching beer. Wood looked up at her and she gave him an almost imperceptible nod.

"All right, I'll keep my ears open," he agreed. By "ears" he meant much more than just the two attached to his own head. He was talking about the ears attached to his street people.

"You realize that the, uh, scene of the crime is a little out of my backyard, don't you?" he added.

"Just a little," I admitted, "but I'm sure that all of your ears don't go deaf once they pass Forty-second Street."

Lee giggled, which was the first audible sound she'd made since bringing out the beer.

"Another beer before you go?" Wood asked, signaling that my "audience" was about over.

I looked down at the bottle I held in my hand, still one-third full, and said, "No more for me, thanks," and put the bottle down on a handy tabletop.

"Lee will show you to the door, Miles. I'll be in touch if I come up with anything you can use."

"Okay, thanks," I said, standing up. Lee slid off the arm of his chair and smoothed her dress over her thighs. She saw where my eyes were and smiled at me. As far as I could tell it was a genuine smile, but it could have been the one she used on her Johns. When she was hooking, she had been extremely good at her work.

Or so I heard.

"This way, Mr. Jacoby," she said, and I started to follow her, which was a pleasant task, indeed. Before we cleared the doorway, Wood called out my name.

"Yeah?"

"It is my humble opinion that you are getting in over your head. Take that for what it's worth, huh?"

I looked at him for a long moment, wondering if he might know more than he was telling, then said, "Sure, thanks."

Just what I needed, a vote of confidence.

CHAPTER FOURTEEN

When I got back to Eddie's office, Missy was gone, but she'd left me a short note.

Dear Jack,
  Don't forget, I get triple time for this.

Missy

The note was a reference to the fact that Eddie always paid her triple time for performance above and beyond, and I guess she figured that this applied. The note was pinned by a paperweight to the top of a high stack of file folders. Next to it was a smaller stack. The higher of the two was marked "Active," the smaller "Inactive." I was going to have to wade through each one of them, but not before I read the copy of the *Daily News* I'd bought on the way over from Wood's place.

Eddie got page five, about four paragraphs' worth, with an accompanying photo of Benny trying to hide his face. The article called Eddie "a small-time private investigator" and Benny "an ex-boxer who was now managing his younger brother's career." It told how Benny had "allegedly" beaten Eddie Waters to death during an argument, apparently using nothing but the "tools of his former trade."

I remembered telling Hocus that I was the fighter in the family and that I didn't think that Benny even knew how to fight. I guess he knew now that was just so much bullshit, or he might have known it all along. Either way, I'd hear about it sooner or later.

I dropped the paper in the wastebasket and then considered my options at that particular moment. I could sit back and examine my own feelings about Benny Jacoby and Eddie Waters, what their relationship was and what the outcome could have been, or I could begin working my way through the folders piled up in front of me and studiously avoid wondering if my brother really could have killed Eddie Waters.

I opened the top folder and began to read.

After three hours I had the folders sorted into three piles. The first was a pile of folders that I had discarded, the second the ones that could be checked by phone, and the third were the ones that I would check personally.

A look at my watch showed that it was now after eleven, too late to do any telephone checks. I wished I could put back the folders I didn't want; but I wasn't all that sure where they went, and I might have just made a bigger mess for Missy to clean up.

I shut the desk lamp and sat there in the dark for a few moments, thinking about Julie and thinking about Benny and Eddie, but always careful to keep them apart in my mind.

I decided that in the morning I'd go down to the morgue to see if I could help Missy make arrangements for picking up Eddie's body. It may seem morbid, but I also wanted to *see* Eddie's body. I wanted to see what my brother was supposed to have done to him. After that I'd see if Missy would do some of the telephone checks for me while I made the personal visits. There were a few rough cases that Eddie had been working on that could have resulted in his death. There were also some dissatisfied customers, but whether they were unhappy enough with his services to want him dead remained to be seen.

It was almost midnight when I left the office, but I still didn't want to go home. I was feeling terribly lonely all of a sudden, and there was no one to talk to. My brother was in jail, my best friend was dead, Packy's was closed, and I didn't dare go and see Julie. I suppose I could have gone to see Tracy again, but as much as she claimed not to be bothered by acting as a substitute, twice in one day might be taxing her feelings a bit.

It was one of those nights that brought home what a small number of friends I really had.

When I stepped out of the building and onto the street, all of a sudden I had more people paying attention to me then I cared to count.

There are considerably fewer rules for street fighting than there are for prizefighting. In fact, there is just one rule for street fighting, which every kid who grows up on the streets of New York learns very well, and that is that there are no rules. So when the first bozo rushed me, I gave him a swift kick in the balls. An act like that inside the ring would have won me a quick trip to the shower, but all I got at that particular moment was a satisfying jolt all the way up my right leg.

I didn't stop to enjoy it, though, because the man on the ground had not come alone. In fact, the second man had been right behind him and had to do a little dance step to avoid tripping over his partner. While he was concentrating on that, I threw a stiff left jab and followed that with a wicked right that put him down for the count.

I had no way of knowing just how many of them there were, but I sensed movement behind me and turned in time to get hit over the left eye with something, some object. I felt my stitches go and the blood run down my face as I hit the concrete. My fighter's instinct kept me going when I should have been knocked out. I rolled when I hit the pavement and kept rolling, still unaware of how many opponents I was dealing with. There were at least three, one of which I knew I'd knocked cold and another who'd be pissing blood for the next few days. I had to keep moving so that the third man couldn't hit me again with whatever it was he'd hit me with the first time.

When I hit the building I staggered to my feet, keeping my back against it, and tried to see through the blood that was covering my face. They weren't coming after me, however. I saw all three of them now, two dragging one, and one of them still crouched over clutching his balls with one hand. I stayed on my feet as long as they were in sight, and it wasn't until they turned a corner that I allowed myself to slide down, back still against the wall, to a seated position.

There was nobody else on the street, or if there was, they were making damned sure they stayed out of sight.

The fact that I was still conscious was due mostly to the pain I was feeling over my left eye. It was bad enough to be keeping me awake. I took out my handkerchief and pressed it to the open wound, and from then on things got kind of fuzzy. The next thing I knew, I was in Bellevue emergency, getting

59

new stitches in my head. I had absolutely no idea how I had gotten there.

"You'll have a headache for a while," I recall the doctor telling me, "but nothing but aspirin and rest will help that. You should be used to that, though, the game you're in."

I said something to him, I don't remember what, and then I remember that it was almost two-thirty in the morning when I left the hospital and headed for home.

I was no longer worried about being lonely. I just wanted to get home and fall into bed.

CHAPTER FIFTEEN

I've never owned a gun, but the following morning I wished I did, because if I had one I would have shot whoever it was that was banging on my door. Every time his fist whacked against my door, the top of my head bounced off and then came back down with a bang.

"Okay, okay," I called out, stumbling and tumbling out of bed. I groped my way to the door, grabbed the knob and pulled it open before I realized that I was totally nude.

"Now, just suppose I was the Avon Lady," Hocus said, looking me up and down. His partner, Wright, was just to his left and behind him, and he smirked at me.

"I wouldn't want any," I told him. "You want to come in?"

"It had crossed my mind," he admitted.

"Okay, so come in," I said, backing up to give them room, "only close the door quietly, okay?"

They entered and Hocus did as I asked, for which I was grateful. "I'm going to have some aspirin," I told them. "Anyone want some?"

"I'll pass," Wright said.

"Yeah, we're on duty," Hocus added.

"That's cute," I said, popping three of the little beggars into my mouth and washing them down with water.

"How about some coffee? I've got instant, and instant."

Wright made a face and put a hand to his stomach, but Hocus said, "As long as it's hot."

I bent to get a pan from beneath the sink and gave a groan when it caused my head to throb more. When I reached above the sink for the instant coffee, I repeated the performance.

"Is this the way you are the morning after all your fights?" Hocus asked.

I got the water and told him, "I didn't have a fight last night."

"Yes," he replied, "you did."

I spooned the instant into two cups and then looked at him. There weren't many places to sit in my two-room apartment—with what they called a kitchenette—but Wright had cleared a chair of my laundry, and Hocus had opted for the bed.

"You heard about that, did you?" I asked.

"Word gets around. Why don't you put on some pants, or something?"

I put on my robe, the one I wore in the ring with "Kid Jacoby" emblazoned on the back in orange letters. By then the water was boiling, so I poured it into the two cups and asked him, "Sugar, milk?"

"Just like that," he said. That was the way I drank mine, too. I handed him his, then took mine back to the sink and leaned against the counter.

"You come to take my complaint?"

He sipped his coffee and shook his head.

"That'd be a waste of paper. What'd you see?"

I shrugged. "I got a real good look at somebody's fist," I told him.

"Want to look at a lineup?" he asked, and Wright laughed.

"Can I get you some juice?" I asked him.

"Got grapefruit?" he asked.

"I think so," I told him. I opened the fridge and checked, found some languishing at the bottom of a bottle for God knew how long and poured it in a glass for him.

"Thanks," he said when I handed it to him.

"Don't mention it."

By that time Hocus had figured out that I was ignoring his lineup line.

"Did you see anyone you knew?" Hocus asked.

"I didn't see anything but—"

"Yeah, I know, 'a big fist.'"

I held my hands apart about a foot and said, "A *big* fist."

"How many were there?"

"Fists?"

"Are you punchy?"

"Only half the time. Okay, there were three that I know of. I came out of the building and something hit me in an unfortunate spot," I explained, pointing to my bandaged head. "I went down, but not out."

"Fighter's instinct, huh? Fight back when you're hurt?"

"You got it. I guess they didn't like it, because they ran off, two dragging one."

"I'm impressed."

"Then you impress easily."

We both finished our coffee at the same time and I asked, "You want another?"

"I don't think I should chance it. Did they make a move to rob you or anything?"

I shook my head. "No, but they might not have had time."

"I guess. Nobody said anything?"

"Not a word."

He stood up and handed me the coffee cup.

"Jacoby, are you snooping around on your brother's behalf?"

"Uh, I've asked some questions, but I wouldn't say that I've been snooping around," I told him, and added to myself, Not yet, anyway.

"You think the attack on me had something to do with my brother's case?" I asked.

He gave a noncommittal shrug.

"You're not convinced that my brother's the killer, are you? Otherwise why would you be here?"

"It doesn't matter whether I'm convinced or not; just because we've got your brother in jail don't mean that I stop investigating," he explained.

"That's a commendable attitude."

"I do think your brother's guilty, though. I just want you to know that."

"Okay," was all I could think to say.

He motioned to his partner, who handed me the glass he'd been drinking before following Hocus.

"Oh, one more thing," Hocus said, letting his partner go out first.

"What's that?"

"If you do decide to do some snooping, do it carefully, huh? Don't go barging in anywhere without thinking first."

"That's number one in Hocus's ten rules of being a good detective?" I asked.

"No," he answered, shaking his head, "number one is never to investigate a case that you're emotionally involved in. Keep in touch, champ."

CHAPTER SIXTEEN

I went back to Bellevue, where I had been treated the night before, but this time, instead of emergency, I went downstairs, to the morgue. I told the clerk there that I wanted to talk to the medical examiner who did the autopsy on Edward Waters.

"That'd be Maybe," the young clerk said, then looked around furtively as if afraid someone might have heard what he said.

"Maybe?" I asked.

"Sorry. I mean Doctor Mahbee. He wouldn't like it if he knew I'd called him that, you know?"

"He won't hear it from me," I promised him. "Can I talk to him?"

"Wait here. I'll see if he's available," he told me. He got up from his reception desk and walked down a hallway. Waiting for him to return, I imagined that I could feel the chill given off by all of the long-dead, cold bodies that were lying down there...somewhere. I had a ludicrous mental image of Dr. Mahbee receiving me in a room full of opened-up bodies, and the chill had crept into my spine by the time the clerk came back down the hall.

"Doc says he can spare you a few minutes," the kid told me.

"Didn't he ask you my name?" I asked.

He shook his head. "No. Seemed to me like he was expecting you? You didn't call ahead?"

It was my turn to shake my head. "No, I didn't."

He shrugged and said, "Well, he said for you to go on back. Second door on the right."

"Okay, thanks."

Dr. Mahbee turned out to be a handsome, East Indian gentleman of about forty years of age.

"You'd be Kid Jacoby," he said to me in perfect English when I entered his office. He extended his hand and I took it.

"How'd you know that?" I asked.

"A friend—er, acquaintance of mine warned—pardon me, advised me that you might be down here sometime today or tomorrow to view the body of Eddie Waters. I understand he was a friend of yours."

"He was. That friend—er, acquaintance of yours, that wouldn't be Detective Hocus by any chance, would it?"

He made a face and said, "The same. It's his case, and he advised me that if you wanted to view the body, I was to allow you to do so."

"Well, that was very nice of him. I would like to look at the body, Doc, if you don't mind."

"Whether I mind or not has no bearing on your request. Come this way, please."

I followed him out through another door and through a couple of partitions to a table covered by a sheet.

"I've done my examination and closed him up already. Still, it won't be a pretty sight," he warned me.

"Go ahead."

He grasped the sheet with one hand and in one motion pulled it off the table, like a magician snapping the tablecloth from a table without disturbing the table settings.

He closed him up all right, and he'd done a nice job of it. The figure-Y incision from the chest to the stomach of the lump of flesh that once was Eddie Waters was neatly stitched closed now.

"I'm in a business where I see lots of stitches, Doc," I told him, "and that's as nice a job as I've ever seen."

He looked at me with his eyebrows raised and then at the sheet in his hand. The fact that I hadn't keeled over in a dead faint seemed to impress him. My stomach should only have been transparent, so he could see what was going on inside.

"Excuse my theatrics, Mr. Jacoby—" he began, but I cut him short.

"That's okay, Doc. Us private eyes are supposed to be hard-boiled, aren't we?"

He didn't answer as I stepped closer to the table to take a good look at my dead friend. A lot of the color had faded from his face, but the swelling and lumps were still visible, evidence that he'd taken a terrific beating before dying.

"What's the official cause of death, Doc?"

"In laymen's terms?" he asked.

"Please."

"He was beaten to death. You can see the marks on his face. What you can't see that I did is the damage that was done to his insides. Somebody who knew exactly what he was doing beat this man until he was dead."

Somebody like a fighter, I thought, or an ex-fighter.

"You can cover him back up now, Doc," I told him. I watched as he meticulously fit the sheet over Eddie's body again, then followed him back to his office.

"Is the body ready to be released?" I asked him.

"As soon as I get word from Hocus," he told me. "Did the deceased have any family?"

"He had a girlfriend," I told him, thinking of Missy. "He always said that she and I were the only family he had. I'll talk to Hocus about sending you the okay. You can release the body to her, but I don't want her to see him. Is that clear?"

"It is. I'll attend to it personally."

I put my hand out and he took it.

"Thanks, Doc. If I need any other information, can I call you?"

"Are you investigating this murder?" he asked.

"I am."

"I was given to understand that there had already been an arrest made."

"That doesn't mean that there's nothing further to investigate," I told him. "I don't happen to agree with the police theory."

"I see. I suppose, then, that if you have need of further information, I would be available—as long as Detective Hocus has no objections."

"I don't think he will," I told him, "but feel free to check it out with him. Thanks again for taking the time to see me."

"No problem, Mr. Jacoby. Good luck with your investigation."

I had said thanks enough times already, so I just nodded

and left. I waved at the kid at the desk on my way out. That chill I'd felt in my spine had spread throughout my whole body by the time I got to the street, and the brightness of the morning sun did nothing to diminish it. I could still see those stitches in Eddie's chest.

And the marks on his face.

The chill came from wondering about who put those marks there, so I stopped wondering.

CHAPTER SEVENTEEN

When I walked into Eddie's office—or what I suppose was my office, at least for the time being—Missy was there on the phone.

"All right, thank you very much. I'm sorry to have disturbed you," she said, and hung up.

"Where have you been all morning?" she demanded. "I've been making calls since I got here."

I walked past her into the main office, and she got up and followed.

"I just came from the morgue," I told her. I sat behind the desk, and she got a good look at my face.

"And they let you go?" she asked. "Why does your face look worse than yesterday, Jack?"

I told her what had happened last night, and she took it well. She was used to it, I guess. Eddie'd taken his fair share of lumps from case to case.

"Were they muggers?" she asked.

"That's the same thing Hocus asked me. As far as I can remember, nobody made a move to try and take anything from me."

"Well, then, why'd they jump you?"

"I don't know, Missy."

"Maybe somebody thinks you're taking over the business?" she offered.

"And that somebody doesn't want me to?" I added.

She shrugged and said, "Could be."

"That means that this 'somebody' could be the same one who killed Eddie," I told her. "Are you admitting that there's a possibility that my brother is innocent?"

"It was always a possibility," she admitted grudgingly.

"Okay," I said, accepting that. I put my hand on a tall stack of files and said, "So we've got a case in here that someone wants closed."

"A needle," she commented, and I had my hand on the haystack.

"You said you've been making calls," I reminded her.

"Yeah, mostly to clients who haven't paid. One or two of them said they weren't satisfied and weren't paying. I've written down their names and addresses for you."

"And the rest?"

"The rest we can cross off. In fact, when some of them heard that Eddie was dead, they offered to send their fee right over."

"What'd you tell them?"

"I told them if they didn't want to pay when he was alive, they could take their money and—"

"I get the picture," I assured her, holding up my hand.

"Are you done calling?" I asked her.

"No, I've got a few more."

"Okay. I'm going to go out and make some personal visits."

"In light of what happened last night," she said, "you might want what's in that bottom right-hand drawer."

I looked at her, then opened the drawer to see what she was referring to.

It was one of Eddie's guns, the .38 Smith & Wesson. I stared at it for a few moments, lying there in its shoulder holster, then slowly slid the drawer shut again.

"I'd shoot myself in the foot," I told her.

"Jack, Eddie didn't like guns either, but there were times when he knew he had to carry one."

"At least he knew what to do with one, if the time ever came when he had to use it. No, I've got these," I told her, holding up my fists, "and they'll have to do. Let me have that list you made."

She handed me a list which had substantially more than the number of names she had originally indicated to me.

"What are all of these names?" I asked.

"I made a list of names and addresses from that pile of

folders," she told me, pointing to the pile I'd had my hand on, "because I knew you wouldn't take the time to do it."

The pile she was talking about were the clients to whom I was planning the personal visits, and she was right, I hadn't thought to write down their names and addresses. That's why she was as good a secretary as she was.

I folded the list and put it in my pocket. My usual attire consisted of a sweatshirt and jeans, but that was my fighter-out-of-the-ring outfit. Today I was wearing my private-eye outfit, which consisted of a sports jacket and slacks, shoes instead of sneakers. The list went into the inner pocket of my sports jacket. I wasn't wearing a tie, because I knew if I did that it would eventually look the way David Janssen's always looked on *Harry-O*. I mean, if it's going to look like that, then why wear a tie?

"If you had looked at it you would have seen that I arranged the list according to address, from the closest to the farthest. You can either work forward or backward."

"I'm starting to get some idea of who really kept this office in shape," I told her, taking the list out again and looking it over.

"Eddie was helpless in the office," she told me. Her eyes misted over a bit, and I was afraid she was going to start crying on me.

"I think you'll find that I'll pretty much follow in his footsteps," I told her. She stared at me for a long moment, then smiled and ran her hand across her eyes.

"Okay, okay, I guess if I carried him I can carry you," she said, and I smiled back at her.

"I'm going to get going on this list," I told her, putting it back in my pocket and standing up.

"Oh, I almost forgot to tell you that you had a phone call," she said.

"You mean, you're human?"

She made a face and said, "Your sister-in-law called."

I froze up and was sure that she noticed.

"What did she want?" I asked, hoping it sounded casual.

"Just wanted to know if you were here. When I told her you weren't, she asked me to give you a message."

"Which is?"

"Just to call her when you can," she told me, looking at me funny. I wanted to get out of there before she started asking any questions.

"If she calls again, tell her I'll be in touch as soon as I can."

"Okay, but—"

"When you're done with all of those calls, you can close up and go home."

"Oh, no. I've got a lot of work to do here. There's still mail coming in, and I've got to straighten the files—"

"Okay, all right, you win. I'll be back later. If anybody calls just take messages, okay?"

"I don't have to be told that," she reminded me.

"I'm sorry, Missy," I told her, meaning it. "Look, if you're still here when I get back, I'll take you out to dinner. How's that sound?"

"We'll see. One of us might have other plans."

Whatever that meant.

"Jack," she called as I headed for the door.

"Yes?"

She made fists and held them up at me, saying, "Keep them up, huh?"

"Don't worry, my guard is always up."

CHAPTER EIGHTEEN

She wasn't there when I got back, so I didn't have to worry about telling her that I was too tired to take her out to dinner. She'd left my messages on Eddie's desk, so I dropped my dragging butt into the chair and started reading.

The first one was from Julie again, with the same message as before, to call as soon as I could.

The second was from Hocus. It said that he had talked to "Maybe"—and she had a question mark after the name—and that we were free to make arrangements anytime.

The third message was from left field—from Willy Wells, the trainer. He wanted me to come by the gym soon as I could.

I put all three messages back on the desk, leaned back and put my feet up next to them. It was almost nine o'clock, and I'd spent the better part of the day talking to people who couldn't have given a shit less that Eddie Waters was dead. I'd talked to four of them, all of whom for one reason or another were displeased with the job that Eddie had done for them. One of them was actually a little upset that he was dead, but only because he had intended to sue him. In every case they were upset because Eddie had done the job they'd hired him to do, but the outcome had not been what they expected, or wanted. You hire a man to find the truth, then condemn him because the truth wasn't really what you wanted at all. You wanted a lie, and you wanted someone else to lie to you and tell you that it was the truth.

Eddie wasn't that kind of a man.

No, none of them were particularly sorry that Eddie was dead, but had any of them had anything to do with his death? I hadn't gotten that impression, as much as I wished I had. They all had alibis for the time of Eddie's death, which I was quite sure would check out. I was going to have their stories checked by one of Eddie's other part-time operatives. Eddie used two other guys once in a while, for tail jobs and serving summonses. I'd call them in the morning and see if one or both of them were willing to do some legwork for me.

I stuffed the messages in my pocket with the intention of answering them, but tomorrow. The only thing I wanted to do right then was get something to eat, and then get to bed.

I walked down to Twenty-sixth Street, between Seventh and Eighth, to a place called Bogie's. They served some of the best Italian food in the city there and offered a Humphrey Bogart motif: posters, stills and a big black falcon behind the bar. The place was run by two friends of mine, Billy and Karen Palmer. They were mystery fans, and the place catered to a large clientele of mystery writers and mystery lovers. On Sunday nights, they played two hours of old mystery radio shows, all from Billy's private collection.

Billy was also into martial arts, holding a third-degree black belt. Karen didn't need martial arts to knock a man flat on his back—she had her looks. She was a lovely brunette who acted as hostess for the place, welcoming people into the place as if she were welcoming them into her own home. Both of the Palmers could have been in their late twenties or early thirties.

When I walked in I saw Billy was doing one of his occasional stints behind the bar. Karen spotted me before he did and came over to give me a big hug. Her hair was up and her shoulders were bare.

"Miles, what a pleasant surprise," she said, squeezing me tightly. I hugged her back, and when Billy looked over and smiled I raised one hand and waved.

"I got an urge for some good Italian food," I told her, "and a big hug from you. I got one, now what about the other?"

"If you get one," she asked, "what do you need with the other?"

"Man's got to eat, Karen," I replied.

She looked around and then said, "Go have a drink at the bar, Miles. I'll have a good table for you in a couple of minutes."

74

"No rush, honey. I'll try to talk your husband into divorcing you so we can get married."

She laughed and went off to get me my table. I went up to the bar, and Billy had a ginger ale standing there waiting for me.

"About time you showed up," he scolded me. "You're the only guy who drinks this stuff."

"How are you, Billy?" I asked, and we shook hands. "How's business?"

"Business is great," he assured me. He was about five nine or so, with a heavy mustache and an easy confidence in the way he stood, the way men who know they can take care of themselves stand. He and Karen made one of the handsomest couples I'd ever seen.

"Miles," he said, putting a hand on my arm, "we were sorry to hear about your brother."

"Thanks, Billy."

"If there's anything we can do, just let us know."

"I'll do that," I said, and drank some of the cold ginger ale. When I put the glass down we started talking about my last fight, and then Karen came over and took me to a table in a corner. She took my order herself, and brought me a plate of the best eggplant parmigiana I'd ever tasted.

"The food just gets better and better," I told both of them after I'd finished. By this time Billy had gotten relieved from the bar, and they both came over and sat with me.

"You should come around more often," Karen told me.

"Come on by Sunday," Billy added, "we're going to play some private-eye stuff."

"I'll try and make it," I promised them.

They were two of the nicest people I knew, Billy and Karen. I paid my check, got another hug *and* a kiss from Karen, and told Billy I'd call him and we'd work out together soon. He told me not to forget about Sunday.

When I left, we all knew that, more than likely, it'd be weeks before I'd get in there again.

CHAPTER NINETEEN

The next morning I decided to answer Willy Wells's message first by going to the gym. The little bantamweight manager-trainer was always the first man in the gym in the morning, getting there even before his fighters. When I got there about ten o'clock, he already had one of his boys working in the ring, and he was shouting orders—not instructions, but orders—at him while he sparred.

"The left, the left, damnit, snap in, don't throw it!" he was shouting.

"You been looking for me, Willy?" I asked, coming alongside him.

He glanced at me, then directed his attention back in the ring.

"Yeah, Kid, I been looking for you," he said from the side of his mouth. "I unnerstand you got a fight coming up in two months with Johnny Ricardi."

He was right. I hadn't thought about that since Benny's arrest, but I did have a fight coming up.

"That's right, so?"

"So," he went on, not taking his eyes off his fighter, "even if your brother is innocent, he won't be back out in time for that fight. You need somebody to get you ready, to work your corner."

"You offering?"

This time he looked at me when he said, "Well, hell, not

77

for nothing I'm offering. I'm saying I'd be willing to take you on—for this one fight—for my usual ten percent."

I thought about it for a moment. As of that moment I had every intention of going ahead with the fight with Johnny Ricardi, and Willy was right—I would need someone to train me and work my corner. The contracts were all signed, so that posed no problem. The economic aspects of the bout were all taken care of. All that remained now was to get in shape and have competent help in my corner.

"Benny still gets his cut," I told him.

"Fine, but mine comes off the top," he countered.

That would be five percent from my cut, and five from Benny's. It was fair.

"It's a deal," I told him. Still watching his fighter, he stuck out his hand and I took it.

"Get changed," he said after that.

"Whoa, wait a minute, Willy. The fight's still two months away and I've got things to do. Besides, I just came out of a fight and I'm in great shape."

"Who told you that? Benny?" he asked. He gave a derisive snort and said, "If you were in great shape, Kid, you wouldn't have had so much trouble with that southpaw."

For the first time since I arrived he turned to me and gave me all of his attention.

"Look, just suit up and get in the ring, go a couple of rounds with my boy, here. I'll tell him not to hit you in the head, so's he don't open that cut again. I just want to get an idea of what you can do."

The name of the kid in the ring was Edwin Lopez, and he was twenty-two. He was one of many comers in Willy's stable, and most of his fights had been televised by one of the national television stations on their "Champions of the Future" series. He had a record of 11–0, with nine knockouts, and he was a welterweight, the division just below mine—unless you counted the nether-divisions, like superwelterweight, or junior middleweight. I didn't. Those divisions were created for those fighters who couldn't compete in the regular divisions, and because somebody figured out a way of making more money by creating junior weight, superweight, and cruiserweight divisions. As far as I was concerned, for all intents and purposes, there were only five major divisions in boxing: lightweight, welterweight, middleweight, light heavyweight, and heavyweight.

None of my fights had ever been on TV, and that had as much to do with my decision to suit up as anything else.

"I'll be ready in a few minutes," I told him.

He started to talk to his boy as I headed for the locker room. As I changed into my trunks, I knew that my pride was making me do this when I should have been out working to clear Benny. Lopez was fast, and he hit hard for a welter. Willy might have had the idea of moving him up to middleweight, and that might have been an ulterior motive for getting me into the ring with the kid. He said he'd have the kid lay off my cut, but I put extra tape and gauze over it, hoping that and the headgear would protect it sufficently. Once I had the headgear in place, I went out so Willy could do my hands.

"All right," he told me while taping my hands, "don't hold back; the kid can take it. I want to see what you can do."

"Okay."

He tied off my gloves and I climbed into the ring. The kid was slick with sweat and he was plenty warmed up. We touched gloves, and he threw a quick jab that hit me on the nose, causing my eyes to water. I backed up and he came with me, throwing two jabs that fell short. My eyes cleared fairly quickly, and when he threw a third jab I stepped by it and hooked a right to the body. He took it well, although I heard him grunt. We bounced around for a while, feeling each other out, but my mind wasn't on it, and I had some trouble breaking a sweat. Willy called time, and we took a breather. The kid listened closely to what Willy was telling him during the rest period, and when we came back to the ring center he threw a jab that landed dangerously close to my cut. I hooked him in the body a couple of times, but I wasn't mad, because I figured it was an accident. The second time could have been accidental also, but not the third, and certainly not the fourth, and then I got mad. I figured he'd go for the cut again, and when he did I sidestepped and double-hooked him in the body, then threw a wicked straight right that caught him flush on the jaw. He backed away, hurt, but he was fast and was able to elude a lot of my follow-up punches. There was no doubt that the kid was good, but I felt that if I could just break a sweat I could get to him. When he hit me on the cut again I felt my face flush with anger, and I started to sweat. After another rest period we came out, and I decided to wait for him to go for the cut again. I caught some punches on my elbows and upper arms, and then he went for it and I nailed him. I hit him two good body shots, and when his hands dropped I nailed him with the straight right hand again; only this time, when he began to backpedal, I didn't let him go. I followed him and nailed him with a wicked left. He lost his balance, and as he was falling I hit him with a cheap shot with the right hand again and almost tore his head off.

"That's it, that's it!" I heard Willy shouting as he jumped into the ring. While he tended to his boy, I spit out my mouthpiece and ripped off my headgear.

"What's the matter?" I sneered at him, "You afraid I'm going to hurt your boy?"

"Hurt him?" Willy said, looking at me over his shoulder. "I'm afraid you'll kill him!"

I hadn't expected that reply, so I just stared at his back as my anger faded. He got the kid to his feet, slapped his face a couple of times, and then told him to go take a shower.

As the kid went to the locker room, Willy turned to me and said, "That kid's never been off his feet, but that's okay. It'll teach him some humility."

"What the hell was the idea, Willy? You deliberately told him to go for the cut!"

"Tell me something," he said as if he hadn't heard me.

"What?"

"How's come you never get that mad in the ring during a fight, hmm?"

"What are you talking about?"

"I've seen most of your fights, Kid. You never get mad at the other guy. You got a bad habit of backing up when you got a guy in trouble. Why is that?"

"Hell, Willy, how do I know?" I answered, amazed at how he had gotten me on the defensive.

"Well, you better find out. You got mad in here today; learn to get mad when you're fighting for real. How long is it going to be before you're ready to go to work?" he asked then, changing speeds on me.

"I'm not sure," I said while he took the gloves off me, "maybe a couple of days, maybe more."

"Okay, just don't develop any bad habits in the meantime. Go take a shower."

I started for the locker room and he called out my name again.

"What?"

"Six weeks," he told me. "I want you six weeks before the

80

fight, Kid, and I don't care what else you got to do. Understand?"

I waved at him and went on into the locker room.

The kid was out of the shower and getting dressed.

"Hey, Jacoby, I'm sorry about the cut, man," he told me.

"That's okay," I told him. I opened my locker and checked out the cut in the mirror on the door. The heavy bandaging had done the job, together with the padding of the headgear. There was a little blood seepage, but the new stiches had held pretty good.

"You know, Willy, he's my man, you know? I got to do what he tells me. No hard feelings?"

He had his hand out, so I took it and said, "Sure, no hard feelings."

As he was ready to leave he said, "You know, you hit pretty hard, man. You not thinking about dropping down in weights, are you?"

"Only if you're thinking of moving up, kid," I told him. He laughed, waved and went out.

Willy Wells was right about my attitude. I couldn't remember ever being as mad in an actual fight as I was in the ring with Edwin Lopez. It was something I was definitely going to have to think about if I intended to stay in boxing.

I put a new bandage on my cut when I got dressed, hoping nothing else would happen to open it again. I wanted it to be cleanly healed for the Ricardi fight. Two months was plenty of time as long as there were no further mishaps.

Before leaving the gym I left three phone numbers with Willy where he could either get in touch with me or leave a message: my home number, the office number, and Julie and Benny's number.

Out on the street I remembered that I still had a message from Julie that needed answering and that I also wanted to call Hocus. On top of that, there was also the list I was supposed to pick up from Dick Gallaghen, the one that would hopefully help me find the man from the fifth row. I decided to go to Gallaghen's office to pick up the list and then make the phone calls from there, also. That is, I'd call Hocus. I'd probably find some excuse for putting off the phone call to Julie just a little bit longer. She'd probably want me to come over and see her, and with my brother out of circulation I didn't really trust myself around my beautiful sister-in-law.

81

CHAPTER TWENTY

"Is he in?" I asked Patrice as I entered Gallaghen's office.

"No, he's at a meeting," she told me, "but he left something for you." She picked up an envelope off her desk top and held it out to me.

"Thanks," I said, taking it from her. "Can I use your phone?"

"For a local call?"

"Of course."

"Sure."

She got up and went into Gallaghen's office, and I perched a hip on her desk and dialed Hocus's number.

"Detective Hocus," he answered.

"It's Jacoby. I wanted to thank you for paving the way with Dr. Mahbee."

"Yeah, no problem. I figured you'd go down there anyway, so I might as well make it easy for you. Maybe give you all the dope?"

"Yeah."

"Good. I've okayed the release of the body. Did Waters have family?"

"Just me and his girl. I'm letting her claim it."

"She won't have any problem."

"Thanks, Hocus."

"Yeah, I'm being nice, Jacoby. You be nice too, huh? Stay out of the way?"

"I'll do my best."

I hung up.

I was pleased that he hadn't told me to stay out of the case entirely, only to stay out of his way, which I fully intended to do. As long as I stayed on his right side, I could count on his cooperation when I needed it. I had no desire to find out just how much of a bastard he could be if I crossed his wrong side.

As I hung up the phone Patrice came back to her desk with a sheaf of papers. I decided to call Julie now instead of putting it off for later. There was no point in avoiding her, since I was the only family she had to turn to with Benny in jail. I would just have to get a choke hold on my feelings.

"One more?" I asked Patrice. She shrugged and waved her hand to indicate that I should go ahead.

I dialed Julie's phone, and she picked up on the first ring.

"Hello?"

"Julie, it's Miles."

"Oh, Miles, hello."

"You called a few times yesterday, but I didn't get back to the office until late. I didn't want to wake you."

"I don't think that's the truth, Miles, but I'll forgive you if you'll come over for dinner tonight. I—I'm not very good at being alone—totally alone, I mean."

The tone of her voice made my throat catch.

"Julie, I'm sorry—"

"Don't be sorry, Miles. Just say you'll come."

I hesitated a moment, then felt ridiculous for doing so.

"Of course I'll come, Julie."

The relief in her voice made my stomach flutter.

"Oh, good. At six."

"Fine. I'll see you then."

"Miles, thank you."

"I'll see you later," I told her, and hung up.

Patrice was watching me, sucking on the end of her pencil. When I hung up she raised her eyebrows and said, "I don't know who 'Julie' is, but I think you've got it bad."

"Don't be silly," I told her, becoming annoyed—at her and myself. "It's my sister-in-law. Naturally, with my brother in jail I'm all the family she has."

"Uh-huh," she said, still staring at me.

"It's only natural that she'd want to—to—"

"Cling to you?"

"Yeah."

We stared at each other a few moments and then she said "Uh-huh" again in that same noncommittal tone.

I gave up and said, "Thanks for the use of the phone, Patrice."

"Sure. Any message for Dick?"

"No—yes. Tell him thanks."

"Okay."

I left without looking at her again. I was afraid she'd still be sucking on that pencil with that knowing look in her eyes.

I hoped she'd swallow her eraser.

CHAPTER TWENTY-ONE

I went to Packy's and sat in a booth with a ginger ale.

I opened the envelope Gallaghen had left for me and found the list I'd asked for. He didn't supply the names of everyone in the fifth row, just the names of the interesting parties. None of them were interesting to me, but what he'd written at the bottom of the page was.

> Jack,
>
> Second name on the list is an old-time manager who still likes to go to the fights—only he wasn't there that night. Somebody was, though, because his ticket was used.
>
> Dick

I checked out the second name on the list: Corky Purcell. An old-time fight manager? How old-time? I didn't remember his name, so it must have been before my time. Maybe he wasn't at the fight, but whoever was might be the guy I was looking for. I needed an address for Corky Purcell, and I thought I knew where to get it.

I went to the bar and asked Packy for his phone. He set it on the bar, and I dialed the number of a friend of mine. Robie McKay was a writer for *Ringtime* magazine, one of the top fight mags in the business. He did an interview with me once, and we got to be pretty friendly.

"Robie, it's Miles Jacoby."

"Fighting Kid Jacoby," he said. That was the title he'd used for the article a year and a half ago. "How ya doing, Kid?"

"Fine, Robie, fine. I—"

"I wasn't at the fight the other night, but I hear you did okay."

"Yeah, when he got tired of hitting me I knocked him cold," I told him.

"That's using your head," he said, then laughed at his own joke.

When he stopped laughing I said, "Robie, I need a favor."

"Ask."

"Does the name Corky Purcell mean anything to you?"

"Purcell," he repeated, "Corky Purcell. No, it doesn't ring any bells. Who is he?"

"An old-time fight manager. Listen, could you ask around down there; maybe some of the old-timers will remember."

Robie was a few years older than me, but it still might have been before his time.

"What info do you need?" he asked.

"I need an address, as current as possible."

"Where will you be?"

"I'll be at Packy's if you get it within the next half hour. After that I'll be around. You can get me at this number after six tonight," I told him, and gave him Julie's number.

"Will I be interrupting anything?" he asked.

"I hope not," I told him, and hung up.

CHAPTER TWENTY-TWO

"Here's your phone, Pack," I told him. He took it and tucked it back behind the bar.

"How's Benny, Jack?"

"Not good, Packy, not good."

"You tell him I was asking about him, all right?"

"I'll tell him, Packy. Give me another ginger ale, will you? No, make it a cream soda; your ginger ale tastes flat."

"I'll give you flat," he retorted good-naturedly, and set a cold bottle of cream soda on the bar.

"I'm waiting for a call, Pack, okay?"

"I'll let you know," he promised.

I went back to the booth and drank my cream soda from the bottle. I looked at Gallaghen's list again, wondering if it would do any good to check out the other names, too. Ah, what's the diff, I figured. There was no hurry, anyway. This was just curiosity. What I should have been doing was something to help Benny, like some more visits to dissatisfied customers of Eddie's. I should probably also have called the office to see if Missy was there. Or was she down at the morgue, claiming Eddie's body?

It didn't matter for now. I had to leave Packy's phone open in case Robie called back, so I drank some more cream soda and waited.

When the half hour was up so was my cream soda, and Robie hadn't called, so I decided to take off.

"I gotta go, Packy. I'll see you around," I called out.

"What do I do if your call comes?" he asked.

"Tell him to use the other number I gave him."

I still had the list that Missy had prepared for me, so I decided to make some more visits before going to Julie's for dinner.

I went to see a man who lived in a penthouse and thought that Eddie should have forced his daughter to come back home after he found her, as he was hired to do. Unfortunately for the man, his daughter was nineteen, and if she didn't want to come home, there was no law in the world that said she had to. Eddie told Papa that the girl was healthy and fine, and that was all he could tell him. She didn't have a permanent address, but Eddie did tell him where she was when he found her. It didn't help the old man, because she was gone from there when he got there. The old guy was pissed good, but enough to kill? I didn't think so.

My second visit was to a man whose wife was missing. It was one of Eddie's failures. He couldn't find her, but he sent the man a bill, which the man refused to pay. He seemed to think that the P.I. business should be run on a no-results, no-fee basis.

I got to Julie's at six-thirty and apologized for being late.

"As long as you're here, Miles," she said, taking hold of my arm and gently pulling me in.

She was wearing a pair of faded jeans and a sweatshirt, no shoes, and her hair was down, hanging to her shoulders. There was no makeup on her face, and she looked tired—but wonderful.

"You look good," I told her.

"Ah, I look horrible," she countered, closing the door.

Something sizzled in the kitchen, and she shouted and ran down the hall. I followed and found her bending over the oven, which was beneath the burners. Her behind looked inviting in those jeans. I felt ashamed for ogling her—but that didn't stop me. When she straightened up and turned around I hurriedly moved my eyes to the stove top.

"What's cooking?" I asked. "Smells good."

"Your favorite," she told me. "Roast chicken, mashed potatoes and plenty of gravy and Italian bread."

"Wow, when do we eat?" I asked, widening my eyes ridiculously.

She laughed and told me that dinner would be served in the

dining room in fifteen minutes. The dining room was a kitchen table with one leg shorter than the others.

"Ah, I left your phone number with someone. I hope you don't mind?"

"Miles, of course not. Relax, will you? I've always wanted you to regard this as your home."

I looked around the rundown little apartment, which seemed even grimmer than my own, and perished the thought. Except for her presence the apartment held no attraction for me.

"Any cream soda?" I asked, opening the refrigerator. It was something I did very easily in front of Benny, but I hadn't done it with Julie in the room. I was trying to force myself to relax with her, and it wasn't easy, not when just looking at her made my hands itch and my teeth ache.

Just then the phone rang.

"Would you get that please, Miles?"

The phone was in the living room, so I walked in there with a large bottle of cream soda in my hand.

"Hello?"

"That you, Jack?" Robie's voice asked.

"Yeah, it's me."

"Am I interrupting anything?"

"No, I haven't started dinner yet."

"Oh," he said, sounding disappointed. "Well, I got your info for you."

"You did? That's great," I said, putting the bottle down and searching for something to write on. I ended up taking Missy's list out of my pocket and writing on the back of that.

"What'd you get?"

"A couple of the old guys down here remember Purcell. He trained a few contenders about thirty years ago. He's about seventy now, goes to the Garden every chance he gets."

"Did you get an address?"

"Yeah, the Roger Williams Hotel, Broadway and Eighty-fourth."

"How recent?"

"A few months ago. He should still be there."

"I hope he is. Thanks, Robie, I owe you one."

"I'll collect," he promised, and hung up.

I tucked the list back into my pocket, picked up the cream soda bottle, and noticed that it had left a wet ring on the end table. I went back into the kitchen and confessed.

"Don't worry about it," Julie told me. "That junk is so old—"

She stopped short, as if she realized that she was about to complain.

"What's the matter?" I asked.

She made a show of tasting the gravy and then said, "Nothing. I don't like to complain."

"Why not? You're certainly entitled," I told her. I went looking for a bottle opener, and she came to help. Up close I could smell her hair, her skin. She wasn't wearing perfume, and what I smelled was simply Julie.

"Here it is," she said, holding up the opener for me. I closed my hand over hers, then took the opener. She went back to the stove and oven.

"It's almost ready," she told me.

The settings were already on the table, so I put down the open bottle of soda and returned the opener to the drawer.

She took out the chicken and shut the oven.

"Would you carve, please?" she asked.

While she dished out everything else I cut the chicken into parts and then put it on the table.

The dinner was strained. No matter how I tried to relax, I couldn't seem to.

"Did you see Benny today?" I asked.

She shook her head slowly.

"No, I didn't—I couldn't."

"Couldn't?"

"Miles, the truth was, I didn't want to."

"Oh."

"Is that all you can say?" she asked.

"You must have had your reasons," I told her.

"Yes," she said, "Yes, I did."

I waited, but they weren't forthcoming.

After dinner I helped her clear the table, and we put the dishes in the sink.

"Just leave them there," she said. "I'll do them later."

"I'll do them," I offered, reaching for the faucet, but she put her hand out to stop me, and we ended up holding hands.

"Julie," I said, wanting to say more.

She tried to pull her hand away, but I held it tight.

"Miles, please—"

"Why did you ask me here tonight, Julie?" I asked.

."What? You're my brother-in-law. I didn't want to be alone. Who else should I have asked?"

"Julie, let's stop playing games," I told her. I pulled on her hand, pulling her toward me. "I can't go on treating you like you were a goddess, or made of glass. I can't go on tippy-toeing around the fact that I'm in love with you."

"Miles—"

I pulled her to me and kissed her, and she responded. Her tongue plunged past my lips and I released her hand and moved my arm around her, pulling her tightly to me. Beneath the sweatshirt she was not wearing a bra, and I reached down and pulled the shirt up to her neck. With one arm around her, I touched her breasts with my free hand. They were warm and full, wonderfully firm, and the nipples sprang to life. As I fondled them she moaned into my mouth.

Suddenly, she put her hands against my chest and pushed me violently.

"Please, Miles—"

"Julie—"

"No, I can't. Not here, not now," she shouted. "Please, just go."

A repeat of the other night, when she had also asked me to leave. She couldn't seem to make up her mind.

"Julie, we have to talk," I told her.

She was crying.

"Not now, Miles, not now."

She ran from the kitchen into her bedroom and slammed the door behind her.

I waited a few moments, and when it became obvious that she was not coming out, I did the dishes and then left.

I went back to my own apartment and began slamming things around. Nothing breakable, just some pillows, some books, a pair of boxing gloves. I had blown it. I'd moved too fast, and now I'd alienated her, just when she needed me most.

Where could she turn now?

I had just taken a bottle of Old Grand Dad out from beneath the sink, with every intention of drinking the whole thing, when someone knocked on my door.

"Shit!" I snapped, wondering who the hell was interrupting my drunk before I could even get started on it.

Whoever it was knocked again, more urgently than before, and I shoved the bottle back under the sink and shouted, "I'm coming, I'm coming."

93

There were three people I might have expected—Hocus, Missy or even Tracy. It was none of the three.

It was Julie, dressed as I had left her, but with a windbreaker over the sweatshirt. Her face was tearstained.

"Julie—"

She sniffled once and stared at me, then said, "I love you too, Miles."

CHAPTER TWENTY-THREE

"Any guilt?" I asked later, while she lay in the crook of my right arm.

"Yes," she answered honestly. "How about you?"

"Tons," I answered just as honestly. Then I asked, "Sorry?"

"No, I'm not sorry, Miles," she told me.

"Good, neither am I. What do we do now?"

She shrugged in the darkness and said, "I don't think we can do anything. I don't think it should happen again."

"I agree," I said, telling her my first lie. Actually, it wasn't exactly a lie. While it was true that it shouldn't happen again, I wanted it to.

And I thought she did, too.

She sat up in bed and I asked, "Where are you going?"

"I've got to go home, Miles. I never should have come here," she told me, but then she touched my face with her hand and said, "but I meant it when I said I wasn't sorry."

I took her hand from my face and held it.

"Julie, what was said—"

"What was said must never be said again, Miles—not for a while, anyway. Not till all this is over with, and Benny is out of jail. Then we can talk about it. I promise you, Miles, my feelings are too deep to just let this go."

"So are mine," I said. I let her hand go and said, "All right. After Benny's out, we'll talk."

"Thank you, Miles."

She dressed in the dark and was careful not to touch me again when she said good night.

"I'm still here, Julie, when you need me."

"I know, and it helps, believe me."

"Are you getting along okay with Heck?"

"Fine, Miles. I trust him."

"Good," I said, "that's good."

"I have to go, Miles. Good night."

"Good night, Julie."

I stayed in bed and listened to her footsteps as she walked to the door and closing it gently behind her went out. I lay back and put my hands behind my head.

At least it was out in the open, my feelings about her, and she had admitted to having feelings for me. I felt like a traitor to Benny, but I was still going to work like hell to prove him innocent, not only because he was my brother—which should have been the optimum reason—but because doing so would mean that Julie and I could sit down and talk.

Sure—get my brother out of jail so I could try and take his wife away from him.

I couldn't sleep, so I got up to make some coffee. As it started perking I thought about Missy and felt guilty about not seeing her or calling her all day. I looked up her home phone in my book and called, but there was no answer. I checked my watch and found that it was only nine-thirty. I'd thought it was later, but it was still too late for her to be out—unless she was on a date, and that was highly unlikely.

I wondered if she'd had Eddie's body moved from the morgue to a funeral home yet, and if so, which one.

Over my coffee I started to wonder if checking out Eddie's clients was going to be a waste of time. None of them so far had seemed homicidal, but what did I know about murder and what kind of people committed murder? Was I kidding myself with this private-eye bit, or what?

I remembered hearing once that a cop was only as good as his contacts. I had contacts. Maybe I wasn't making the best use of them.

I picked up the phone and dialed Knock Wood Lee's number. Tiger Lee answered.

"Is he in, Lee?"

"To you? Probably, but let me ask."

Complete silence and then Wood came on the line.

"What's up, brother?"

"That's what I want to know from you, Wood. You get a line on what we talked about?"

"I think so, but it wasn't solid, so I didn't call you. I'm checking it out further."

"What have you got so far?"

"Well, there is some imported talent in town, that much I know," he told me.

"Imported talent? You mean hit men?"

"Hey, if you're gonna work this side of the street, brother, you're gonna have to learn the lingo. Yeah, that's what I mean, Miles, only in this case it's hit *man*, singular."

"Well, who's his target?" I asked eagerly. "Was it Eddie?"

"That's what I'm checking further," he told me.

"What about his name, where he's staying?"

"Miles, look, one of my ladies saw the guy in town and recognized him. She knows he's a button man, but she couldn't remember his name. I'm trying to get a line on who he is and where he's staying, but I don't want that line traced back to me. Do you understand what I'm saying?"

"Yeah, I understand. You're going slow and careful."

"You got it. Last thing I need is some mechanic finding out I'm trying to track him down."

"Okay, Wood, I know you're taking a chance. I appreciate it. Just call me as soon as you have something, okay?"

"Miles, I think you're barking up the wrong tree."

"That's a cliché I always hated, Wood. What do you mean?"

"Well, from what I hear, Eddie was beaten to death, right?"

"Right."

"I don't know any mechanics who work that way. It's sloppy, it's not sure—"

"It's all I got, Wood. Just let me know, okay?"

"You got it, brother. You'll be the second to know, after me," he promised.

"Okay, Wood, thanks."

"Hey, you sound down, man. Want me to send a lady over?" he offered. If I thought he was offering me Tiger Lee, I just might have said yes.

"No thanks, Wood. Maybe next time," I told him, and hung up.

I wondered if Hocus knew that there was a "button man" in town. If he did, what would he do about it? More importantly, now that I knew, what was I going to do about it?

What I did was pour half a cup of coffee down the drain

and go back to a bed that was still warm from her and still smelled like her.

What I did was spend a pretty restless night, for more reasons than one.

CHAPTER TWENTY-FOUR

In the morning I went to the Roger Williams Hotel to look for Corky Purcell.

I grabbed the IRT No. 3 express to Seventy-second Street, then switched to the No. 1 local to Eighty-sixth. The hotel was on Broadway between Eighty-fourth and Eighty-fifth streets. Eighty-fourth Street was also called Edgar Allan Poe Street, and they held street fairs there every year to celebrate Poe's birthday—or so I'd heard.

The Williams was a bit of old New York. Most of its former glitter—in fact, all of it—was gone now, but it did maintain a sort of seedy, faded class, and still had not sunk to housing drunks and derelicts.

The desk clerk was busy mourning the latest collapse of the Mets defense, and when I asked him what room Corky Purcell was in, he didn't even look up from the box score when he told me Room 502, on the fifth floor.

"Thanks," I told him. He didn't answer. He was back crying over another Taveras error and three more Kingman strikeouts.

I took the creaky, coffin-box elevator to the fifth floor and swore I'd take the stairs back down when I was finished. I decided to look at it as an early start in my training for the Ricardi fight, rather than admit to myself that I was afraid to get into that damned thing for the trip back down.

There was loud music coming from behind the closed door

of one of the rooms, and it wasn't until I located Room 502 that I realized that it was coming from there.

I knocked on the door and got no answer. Figuring that the loud music was keeping him from hearing my knock, I began to pound on the door with my professional right. The results were quick and totally unexpected, catching me off guard.

The door opened inward and two men came running out. They both barreled into me, driving me back against the door opposite 502. I hit it fairly hard and the air was temporarily driven from my lungs. By the time I recovered they had already hit the stairs, and I debated whether to follow them or go into the room on the chance that someone might need some help.

As it turned out I should have followed them. Not that there wasn't someone in the room; it was just that he wasn't in any particular trouble at that moment—and he would never be again.

He was dead.

I had to assume that the little man on the floor was Corky Purcell. He was lying on his back, and his eyes were open, staring sightlessly at the ceiling. The smell of burnt flesh was sharp in the air, and I could see that his feet were bare and the soles had been burnt in several places with either a cigarette or a cigar. Apparently they were after some information from the dead little man, and I wondered if it had anything to do with the reason I was there, too.

I walked over to the radio on the dresser, which was still blasting out rock music, and shut it off. Then I picked up the phone and dialed 911. I told the girl who answered that I wanted to report a homicide.

"A dee-oh-aye?" she asked me.

"No, sweetheart, a hom-i-cide," I replied sweetly. I asked her to please have the proper people respond and gave her the location. She also asked me for my name and the phone number of where I was calling from, and then said she'd send a car right over. I hung up hoping I'd never really need help from the police and have to rely on 911.

I called the desk clerk downstairs and told him that the police would soon arive and would he send them right up to Room 502. He said he would and hung up. I thought it odd that he didn't ask me what had happened, but maybe he wasn't finished reading about the Mets.

When I was finished with the phone I knelt down by the little man on the rug. Aside from being burned, he'd also been beaten about the face, though not too severely. It looked as if they had simply wanted to get his attention before they started questioning him.

About what?

"What did you know that got you killed, Corky Purcell?" I asked the body, but he didn't answer. He just kept staring up at the ceiling. I would have liked to close his eyes for him, but I didn't want to touch the body at all until the cops got there.

When the first radio car arrived I identified myself to the two cops by showing them my P.I. ticket, and then told them what had happened, as far as I knew.

One of them bent down and looked at the body, then stood up and told his partner, "You better put in a call for the squad, Tommy."

"Right," his partner replied.

The first one was wearing a name tag that said Parlato. His partner's said Plunkett.

Plunkett turned to me and said, "You'll have to stick around and talk to them."

"No problem," I assured him.

While Plunkett made the necessary requests over the radio— the squad, the duty captain, the sergeant on patrol, the medical examiner—Parlato asked me, "You carrying a piece?"

"A piece of what?"

He frowned at me and said, "A gun, pal."

"No," I told him, shaking my head, "no gun."

"You mind?" he asked, motioning with his hands for me to raise mine so he could frisk me. I complied, and he satisfied himself that I was unarmed.

Plunkett had walked over to the window to transmit his requests, and upon completion of his transmission he rejoined his partner and me.

"Homicide's on the way," he told Parlato, "along with a wagon and the M.E. The boss will probably get here first."

"Good," his partner replied.

At that point the sergeant walked in, followed closely by the captain. The others began to arrive, and from that point on things got kind of confused. I got shuffled off into a corner while they rushed around, bumping into each other at every opportunity.

It was wonderful watching the law at work.

CHAPTER TWENTY-FIVE

When the detectives arrived I was surprised to see that it wasn't Hocus and his partner. The two men who did show up were strangers to me.

"You the guy who found the body?" one of them asked.

"That's right," I told him. I showed him my ticket and said, "My name's Jacoby."

He handed it back to me and his partner asked, "Are you Kid Jacoby?"

"That's right."

"I saw you fight the other night," he told me.

"Did you?"

"Yep. You were lucky to get out of that ring with your head still attached."

"So I've been told," I replied sourly.

They introduced themselves as Detectives Vadala and D'Elia. Which was which didn't really matter, as they were almost interchangeable. Both about the same height and build, both snappy dressers, unlike Hocus and his partner, who always looked like they got dressed in the dark.

For purposes of identification, Vadala had a full head of salt-and-pepper hair, and his partner had thinning brown hair.

"Somehow I thought Hocus would get down here for this," I told them.

Vadala seemed to take that as a slam against him.

"Hocus can't catch every case that comes along," he told me. "You a friend of his?"

I shook my head.

"We're working on a couple of things at the same time," I told him.

"Together?"

"Not necessarily."

While D'Elia went over to speak to the first two officers on the scene, Vadala told me, "You'll have to come downtown to sign a statement, but why don't you give me your story now?"

I told him that I was looking for Corky Purcell, had received information that he was registered in this hotel, and what had happened after I arrived and knocked on his door.

"Why were you looking for him?" he asked.

"I wasn't really looking for him. I'm looking for someone else, and I was hoping that Corky Purcell could lead me to him."

"Who you looking for?"

"I don't know his name," I told him.

"Are you being straight with me?" he demanded suspiciously.

"As straight as I can," I told him. I just wasn't being very clear, but that was his fault. I didn't like the way he came on.

He walked over to the body and said, "So this is Purcell?"

I shrugged.

"I don't know. I never met the man before."

"You're not being very helpful," he complained.

"Look, I'm perfectly willing to come to your office to make a statement, but you're going to be here awhile. Why don't I come by later in the day. Maybe by then I'll know more, so I can tell you more," I suggested.

I knew his first inclination was to keep me right there until he was finished, but he seemed to think better of it.

"All right, Jacoby. Come down to the Seventeenth Precinct around five this evening. I go off at six."

"I'll be there."

I started for the door, then stopped short and said, "There is something that might help."

"What?" he asked.

"You might ask the desk clerk why he knew what room Purcell was in without looking it up and why he wasn't curious at all about why the police were coming."

It was kind of a show of good faith on my part, and he said, "I will, thanks."

I waved and left.

I was hoping to get a chance to talk to Hocus before five, or at least see him as well as Vadala at that time. I wondered if I could get him to work on this case along with Benny's. I thought I might get more cooperation from him than I would from Vadala.

One of the first things I wanted to find out from Hocus was what had killed Corky Purcell—if the dead man was Purcell. Other than the burn marks on his feet and the bruises on his face, there wasn't another mark on him that I could see.

Out on the street I got away from the crowd of police vehicles parked in front of the hotel and found a pay phone. I had suddenly remembered that Heck Delgado had asked me to call him, and that was two days ago.

I dropped in a dime and dialed his number.

"I'm sorry, Mr. Jacoby, but Mr. Delgado is in court," his secretary told me. "May I take a message?"

I told her to tell him that I apologized for not having called earlier and that I'd keep calling in periodically until I got him. I asked her if she had any idea when he'd be back, but she said he could walk through the door any minute or not get back at all. I thanked her for her help and hung up.

Next I called Missy at the office. It wasn't Eddie's office anymore, and I couldn't think of it as mine, so it was just "the office."

"How're you doing?" I asked her.

"Fine," she said, sounding anything but.

"I tried to call your house last night, but you weren't home," I told her.

"I went to my mother's and spent the night there. I didn't feel like being alone," she answered. "I saw him, Jack, and that kind of made it too real, you know?"

Damn that M.E. I had asked him to make sure she didn't see Eddie's body. Ah, I guess I couldn't blame him.

"Guess I can't blame you," I told her. "Feeling alone is a scary thing. Next time call me, huh?"

I thought I detected a smile in her voice when she said, "Thanks, friend. I'll remember."

"Still making phone calls?" I asked.

"Yes, that and getting the office in order. Anything to keep me busy."

"I've got something that should keep you busy," I told her. "Dig up whatever you can for me on an old fight manager and trainer named Corky Purcell. Newspaper articles, magazine pieces, anything. Call Robie McKay at *Ringtime* magazine and tell him I need another favor. Talk nice to him; you know how to do it."

"Yeah, I know how," she said, and she left the rest unsaid. The part that goes "but why should I?" She knew that Purcell had nothing to do with Eddie's killer, but still she didn't say it. Instead she said, "I should know how, I had a good enough teacher."

"You had the best, kid. We both did," I told her. "Hey, I should be in a little later. If you're still there I'll take you out for a bite."

"Promises, promises. We'll see."

"Okay."

"Miles?"

I had almost hung up, but I put the phone back to my ear.

"Yeah?"

"The funeral's tomorrow."

"Yeah," I said, and after a pause, "okay."

"You will be there, won't you?" she asked.

"Of course I'll be there," I told her. "You better write down the address, though, just in case you're gone when I get back."

"All right, but I'll be leaving late."

"Okay. I'll see you later."

I hung up the phone and stood there with my hands still on the receiver. I looked down the block to where the police cars were still parked, their turret lights flashing red and white. With Purcell dead, my only link to the man in the fifth row was gone. I should probably have abandoned my search at that point and just concentrated on Benny's case, but the way Purcell had died wouldn't let me do that.

I had given the first officers on the scene whatever description I could of the two men, but our "encounter" had been so fast and unexpected that I knew I would never be able to recognize either one of them even if I were in an elevator with them.

Had they been there to question Purcell, to kill him, or both? And if it were the latter, then how did they do it? If they were there to question him, what did they want to know?

Could they have been after the same thing I was?

Interesting questions, to say the least, and my curiosity wouldn't allow me to forget them, or Corky Purcell.

I stopped leaning on the phone and walked over to catch the subway back downtown. There were two things I particularly wanted to get done that day. I wanted to talk to both Hocus and Heck.

I wanted to try and get Heck to use me as his investigator on Benny's case. I knew he had his own men, but it hadn't been unusual for him to use Eddie on occasion.

As far as Hocus was concerned I wanted to find out if he had come up with anything on Benny's case. I also wanted to make sure he'd let me know what the autopsy on Corky Purcell came up with.

You get a lot of time to think while you're riding the subway, and when you're through thinking about the things you want to think about, you start thinking about the things you don't want to think about. I got off the train at Times Square and continued downtown on foot. Watching the girls and watching out for the cars kept my mind nice and busy, and by the time I reached Fourteenth Street the depression I'd developed from thinking about the things I didn't want to think about had disappeared.

CHAPTER TWENTY-SIX

I stopped in at the Arthur Treacher's at Fourteenth Street and Union Square for some chicken and chips, the first junk food I'd had since going into training for my last fight. I'm a junk-food freak, and the only time I get to eat it is between fights.

After lunch I dropped another dime into one of Ma Bell's one-armed bandits and called Heck's office again. His secretary told me he was in and would be for some time. I told her I'd be there in ten minutes.

Heck's office was on Madison and Twenty-third, so I walked back uptown nine blocks and took the elevator up. When I walked into his office the secretary told me to go right in. I didn't recognize her, which wasn't surprising. Heck had the knack of having a different young woman out front every time I was there. I didn't know if he fired them or they quit, but there was no denying he had a large turnover of personnel.

"I expected you to call sooner, Miles," he told me, as if he was disappointed in me. He looked up from his desk, and when he saw my face had picked up a few extra lumps he said, *"Madre de Dios,* pal!"

I told him about being jumped on the street, and then about jumping into the ring with Willy Wells's boy.

"Well, at least one of those incidents was unavoidable," he commented.

I grinned sheepishly and said, "Yeah, I know. Don't worry, I don't intend to get into the ring again until my eye heals."

"That's good. What about this attack on you? Do you think it had anything to do with your brother's case?"

"Maybe not directly," I told him.

"What do you mean by that?"

I sat in his visitor's chair and said, "I've been checking out Eddie's clients, to see if maybe one of them had a motive for wanting him dead."

"And? You found something?"

"I haven't found a blessed thing," I told him, "but on the other hand, maybe someone thinks I have."

He thought it over a moment, then said, "I think I understand. Either someone thinks you have something or there is something they don't want you to find. That's why they sent those two *cabrons* after you."

"What's that word?"

"It's a dirty Spanish word, Miles."

"Oh, well, that's the way I figure it. It would have been more helpful if those two, uh, goons had spoken to me or given me some kind of warning or something."

"You mean like on the television, when the villain tells the hero, 'Stay away from so-and-so,'" he said, dropping his voice to a dramatic, villainous level, "and then the detective knows who to look for?"

"Right. I guess that would have been a little too much to hope for, huh?"

"Maybe you didn't give them a chance to talk," he suggested. "Perhaps they didn't expect you to fight back so effectively."

It was my turn to think one over.

"Well then, maybe they'll try again, and I will get a warning," I offered.

"Or maybe next time they'll just kill you."

"Oh, now that's a cheerful thought. Thanks a heap."

"I'm sorry, Miles, I did not mean to alarm you. Perhaps they were just muggers."

"Yeah, maybe," but I didn't think so. I shifted uncomfortably in my chair and asked, "Heck, how are you progressing on Ben's case?"

"Not very well, I'm afraid," he answered. "He refuses to change his story at all."

"Have you got anyone working on it?"

"Yes, I have Walker Blue doing some investigative work for me. He went through the office building, found a couple of people who remembered seeing your brother that day."

"In what kind of shape?"

"Inebriated, to say the least," he replied helplessly. "There's no avoiding that fact, Miles."

"I know it, but that doesn't prove he killed Eddie," I pointed out defensively.

"No, it just proves he was there, which is half the state's case."

"He's not denying that he was there, Heck!"

"Easy, Miles," he said, holding up both hands so I could see the palms, "don't jump on me."

I sat back in my chair and apologized.

"I'm sorry, Heck. Listen, why don't you let me work on this thing, too?"

"Walker likes to work alone, Miles, and besides, you're a little emotionally involved—"

"Emotionally and financially," I told him.

He frowned and asked, "How is that?"

"Well, Ben sure hasn't got any money to pay you."

"Thanks for telling me," he said wryly.

"Oh, don't worry, Heck, I can pay you."

"I'm not worried, Miles," he assured me. "Look, you know Walker Blue's a good man—"

"I know, but he's not cheap. I am," I countered.

"Now you are going to tell me that you are trying to save yourself some money by working on the case yourself, right?"

"Right."

"That's a good try, Miles," he complimented me.

"Look, Heck," I tried again, "I'm going to nose around anyway, but it would help if I had some kind of official capacity, just in case push comes to shove with the cops. Put me down on the books and pay me a dollar. I just want to be able to tell them I'm working for you."

He cocked his head to the right and asked, "Have you had any trouble with the police?"

"No. I've met the detective in charge—"

"Hocus?"

"Right. We seem to be getting along so far, but I'll need a leg to stand on if he tries to warn me off."

He thought it over a moment, then said, "All right, Miles, I may be wrong, but you're hired."

"Thanks, I appreciate it—and since I'm more than likely paying the bills, I compliment you on good judgment."

"Thank you," he said, bowing his head.

"I guess I'll get to work, then," I said, starting to rise.

"Oh, there's one more thing, Miles," he commented, stopping me.

"What's that?" I asked, half in and half out of the chair.

"Your brother wants to know why you haven't been to see him in the past few days."

I was suddenly struck by guilt over what Julie and I had done last night, and I sat back down.

"Tell him they won't let me in to see him," I suggested.

He shook his head.

"As an investigator working for his attorney, they can't stop you from seeing him," he advised me, sounding very officious.

"Yeah."

"How about tomorrow morning," he suggested. "You can go in with me."

"Is Julie going?" I asked.

He shook his head.

"She'll be going in the afternoon."

He was wondering why I wasn't in a hurry to visit my brother, and, to be truthful, I was wondering the same thing. It wasn't because of what happened with Julie, because I hadn't been in such a rush even before that. Part of it was probably because I was just tired of taking care of someone who had for years been pretending he was taking care of me. The other part might have been because, damnit to hell, he just might have—I mean it *was* possible that he had killed the best friend I ever had. Maybe I thought that by not seeing him, not looking at him, I could go on believing that he hadn't killed him, in spite of all the evidence.

"Miles," Heck called out, breaking into my reverie.

"Yeah, Heck, I'm here."

"Miles, I don't know what the problem is, so I can't tell you how to solve it, but he *is* your brother."

I looked at him and grinned slightly.

"Is that Latin logic?" I asked.

He smiled widely and said, "That's just the truth."

"Yeah," I admitted, scratching my nose, "I guess it is that. Okay, Heck, I'll go with you tomorrow."

"Good. Meet me in front of my office at ten o'clock in the morning, and we'll go out to *Ryker's Island* to see him."

I got up to leave and then thought of something else I should bring up.

"Heck, there is something that you should know about," I said, turning back to him.

I told him all about Corky Purcell, why I was looking for him, and how I found him.

"You think the murder of this Purcell has anything to do with Ben's case?" he asked. "I fail to see the connection."

"Well, so do I," I told him. "I think it might have something to do with the man in the fifth row, though. Since I'm working for you, I just thought you should know everything I was working on."

"Fair enough," he agreed. Pointing his finger at me, he added, "You let me know the minute you come up with something I should know, though."

"Believe me, you'll be the first to know," I promised.

CHAPTER TWENTY-SEVEN

I went straight from Heck's office to the Seventeenth Precinct. I was deliberately trying to avoid Detective Vadala, at the same time hoping that Hocus would be in and would take my statement instead.

When I walked into the Precinct I was stopped by an officer at the front desk who wanted to know where I thought I was going.

"Homicide," I told him.

"Do you have an appointment?" he asked.

"I, uh—yeah, I do."

"Who with?"

"Detective Hocus."

"Stand by," he told me, picking up a phone. He spoke briefly, casting suspicious glances at me, then hung up and said, "All right, you can go up."

"Thanks."

"Next time stop at the desk and identify yourself or mention if you have an appointment."

I bit back a coarse reply and said, "I'll remember, thank you."

He didn't answer. I had already ceased to exist as far as he was concerned.

I went upstairs and was met at the door to the squad room by Hocus.

"I hear you were involved in some excitement uptown," he said by way of greeting.

"Yeah, I came down to make my statement."

"Well, Vadala's not back yet, but you can come in and wait for him," he offered.

"Thanks."

He led me inside, and instead of going to his lieutenant's office he took me to his desk.

"How have you been doing with my brother's case?" I asked him as he seated himself.

"Well, I haven't found anything to make me change my mind about him, if that's what you mean," he answered honestly.

"Yep, that's what I meant," I said, looking around the room.

There were eight desks, only three of which were inhabited now. At one a lone detective sat laboring over a typewriter. At the other another detective sat with an elderly woman, showing her photos. The third desk was Hocus's.

"Why don't you have a seat," he invited, indicating the one next to his desk.

"Thanks."

"Can I get you a cup of coffee?"

"No, thanks," I told him, sitting down. "Uh, listen, would it be possible for you to take my statement?"

"Um, it's not my case, but I guess I could take your statement, yeah. Are you in a hurry?"

"It's not that I'm in a hurry," I told him, "as much as it is that I want you to hear the story."

"Oh? Why's that?"

"Well, you're working on the Lucas Pratt case, right?"

"Right," he said. Then leaning forward, he asked, "You think there's a connection?"

"I . . . think you better take my statement and then decide for yourself."

Half an hour later he was glancing over my typewritten statement, nodding his head.

"Is that enough of a connection for you to take over the Purcell case?" I asked. "Both Lucas Pratt and Corky Purcell could have led me to my man in the fifth row—"

"And now they're both dead," he finished for me. He let my statement flutter to his desk and added, "Yeah, that's a connection, all right. Vadala may not like it, but I'm pretty sure I can get the boss to turn the case over to me."

116

"Great."

"Why are you so enthusiastic?" he wanted to know.

"I just think that I can get along with you better than I can with Detective Vadala," I told him.

He frowned at me.

"Jacoby, are you going to continue with your search for the man in the fifth row?"

"I am."

"Uh, does that mean that you're not going to work on your brother's case?"

"No, it doesn't. As a matter of fact, I've been retained by Hector Delgado to do some background investigation on the case."

"Is that a fact?" he asked, very interested. "Correct me if I'm wrong, but your sister-in-law hired Delgado on your recommendation, didn't she?"

"That's right."

"Yeah, well," he said, picking the statement up off the desk, "I guess that means you've got almost as much right on the case as I have."

"I don't see any reason why we can't work together," I told him. "You know, exchange information."

"I'm glad to hear you say that, Jacoby. We both want the same thing, right?"

"But for different reasons."

"Well, whatever the reason, we want the guilty party to be punished. The best way to do that is for you to clue me in on anything you find out."

"And vice versa."

"Yeah, right."

I stood up and told him. "I'd like to call you tomorrow and find out what the autopsy report says about Purcell and the cause of death. I didn't see any marks on him that would have killed him."

"I should have the report by tomorrow morning, so sure, give me a call."

"I'm going to see my brother at ten," I told him. "I'll call you after that."

I started to walk out and he called after me.

"Jacoby."

"Yeah?"

"You let me know if you find your man in the fifth row.

He could be more than the connection between these two cases," he told me.

"What do you mean?"

"Maybe he doesn't want to be found," he suggested. "Just maybe he's the killer."

CHAPTER TWENTY-EIGHT

As I left the Precinct I was struck by the fear that I might meet Detective Vadala on his way in, but mercifully that fear did not materialize into reality. No doubt he would be informed by his superior that the Purcell case was being turned over to Hocus due to certain similarities, or connections, with one of his cases. It would serve no good purpose for him to find out that I had something to do with it. The last thing I needed if I was going to stay in this business was a cop with a grudge.

I walked downtown to the office and arrived there just before six o'clock. Missy was hanging up the phone when I walked in.

"Ready to eat?" I asked her.

"Well, well, a man who keeps his promises," she said, slapping her hands down on the folders that covered the desk. "Shall I tell you want kind of day it's been now, or over dinner?"

"Let's make it over dinner," I told her, realizing how hungry I was. "I'm starved."

We decided against anything fancy and simply went to the nearest Brew & Burger.

Once we had a couple of giant burgers, a mound of French fries and a carafe of wine in front of us, she started telling me what kind of day it had been.

"So you spoke to a lot of nasty people, but no one you think might have had a reason to kill Eddie," I summed up.

"Yeah, they were nasty, but so are ninety percent of the people in New York. That doesn't make them murderers."

"I guess not."

"How was your day?" she asked.

"It started off great," I told her, then related my story about finding Corky Purcell's body and just kept on going to bring her up to date.

"That reminds me," she said when I finished. "Your friend Robie McKay is sending an envelope full of clippings over in the morning."

"He come on strong on the phone?" I asked, smiling.

She didn't smile back when she answered.

"Yeah, but I cooled him off without hurting his feelings," she told me, playing with her French fries with her fork. Her burger was only half gone, but she was doing a dandy job on the wine.

"Hey, kiddo, what's on your mind?" I asked her.

She poured herself some more wine and picked up her glass.

"You are," she said. "Why are you so interested in an old-time trainer who turns up dead in a rundown hotel? Does it have anything to do with getting your brother off the hook for Eddie's murder? Does it have anything to do with Eddie's murder at all?" she demanded.

"No, not with Eddie or my brother," I admitted.

"You going to keep the business open, then?" she asked. "You taking on other jobs already?"

"No, this is personal. It started before Eddie was killed, or Ben was arrested," I told her, and went on to explain it all to her so she wouldn't think I was cutting out on my brother, or trying to cut in on Eddie's action now that he was dead. I understood that it was the wine talking, because she knew me better than that.

"Missy, I know this is hard for you—" I started.

"Hard? You don't know the half of it," she told me. "Miles, I still think your brother killed Eddie. You haven't come up with anything that's changed my mind. Have you changed yours? Have you come up with anything at all that proves your brother didn't do it?"

I hesitated a moment and then admitted, "No, nothing."

"Then why don't you forget it, Miles?" she asked. "The police have Eddie's killer."

"He's my brother, Missy; that's the only justification that I can give you."

120

She regarded me for a moment, then set the wineglass down while it was still half full and threw a disgusted glance at it.

"Do you have anything at all?" she asked.

"The only thing I've got that stands out is that there's a hit man in town. Who he is, exactly who he's after, I don't know yet."

"I never saw a hit man who worked with his hands, Jack," she told me. She'd gone back to calling me Jack, instead of Miles, which I considered a good sign. "It's usually a knife, or a gun, or some other weapon, but never his bare hands."

"There's always a first time," I told her.

"Remember what Eddie used to say, Jack?" she asked me. "Consider every possibility, but don't reach, don't stretch for it. You're reaching, Jack."

"Maybe I am," I conceded, reaching for my wineglass.

She reached out and covered my hand with hers. I looked at her face and she smiled.

"I'm sorry I snapped at you, Jack. It's just that—with the funeral tomorrow, I'm—"

"It's all right," I assured her. "We're friends, Missy. If you can't snap at me, who can you snap at?"

She squeezed my hand and said, "Thanks."

After dinner I asked her if she wanted coffee, and she said no, she just wanted to go home.

"Do you want me to come with you?" I asked.

"Is that a proposition?" she asked.

"Hardly," I told her. "Another time maybe, but I've got enough problems right now as it is."

"Lady problems?" she asked.

"A lot of problems," I replied very deliberately.

"Okay, none of my business," she said.

We stood up and she wobbled a bit.

"Why don't you take a cab instead of the train?" I suggested.

"Maybe I will," she agreed.

Outside I whistled and shouted myself hoarse and finally was able to flag down a cab.

"Queens," she told the driver when she got in. "I'll give you the address when we get over the bridge."

"You got it, pretty lady," the driver said. He was fat and sixty, so the remark seemed innocent enough.

"I'll see you tomorrow, Missy," I told her.

"I left the location on your desk, Jack. I'll see you there," she replied. "Good night."

It wasn't until the taillights of the cab had faded from view that I realized what she had said.

She had left the location on "my" desk.

CHAPTER TWENTY-NINE

I walked back to "my" office and sat down at "my" desk.

I was trying the "my" on for size, and I was finding that I liked the fit.

Sitting behind the desk, I felt that Eddie would want me to keep the business going. If I decided to do that, my other problem would be whether or not to keep on fighting.

Save it, I told myself; save any major decisions until your mind is clearer. Find Eddie's killer first, or at least prove that Benny couldn't have done it.

Where was the higher priority, I then asked myself. What did I want to do, find Eddie's killer or get Benny out of jail? I guess I'm a glutton, but I wanted both. One wouldn't satisfy me.

Eddie was my best friend, and to leave his killer walking around thinking he'd gotten away with it would just grate on me for the rest of my life. Benny, on the other hand, was my brother. He was a drunk, he was a pain in the ass, and he was married to Julie—which was probably the biggest thing I had against him—but he was my brother, my only living blood relative, and I couldn't just let him rot in the slammer without trying to do something about it. If it turned out that he was guilty . . .

Well, that was different.

Missy had laid it right on the line, whether it was influenced by the wine or not: Had I found anything to prove that Benny hadn't killed Eddie?

No! Not a blessed thing!

The only thread I had to grasp at was the hit man that one of Wood's girls had seen in town. Why was he here? Who was he after? Had he made his move already by killing Eddie, or was he here for a totally different reason?

I should have mentioned that to Hocus, damnit, to see if he knew anything about it.

I picked up the phone and dialed his number.

"Detective Wright, Homicide," his partner answered.

"Wright, this is Jacoby."

"Oh yeah, the champ. What's up?"

"Is Hocus around?"

"No—wait a minute, yeah, there he is. Hold on."

I held on for a few seconds, listening to the squad-room sounds until Hocus came on the line.

"What's up, Jacoby? You find out something already?" he asked.

"No, it's something I already knew but forgot to mention."

"What's that?"

"Do you know anything about a hit guy being in town?"

"Who?"

"I don't know."

"From where?"

"I don't know that either."

"That's not much to go on," he told me.

I explained that I had a source who said that they had seen someone in town whom they knew was a hit man, but they couldn't remember the guy's name, or where they had seen him.

"Your informant seems to have a very selective memory," he observed.

That stopped me because he was so right, and I had never thought of it that way.

"Yeah, it sure sounds that way," I told him.

"Look, check it out a little further and then call me back. It could be something we should look into."

"I'll get back to you," I told him, and hung up. I picked up the phone and dialed again, this time calling Wood.

Tiger Lee answered.

"Is he in, Lee?"

"How come you never want to talk to me?" she asked, flirting.

"When your phone number is different from his phone number, I'll call to talk to you," I promised.

124

"Coward. Hold on."

In a few seconds, Knock Wood Lee came on the wire.

"I can't tell you anything I didn't tell you last night, Jack," he said. "Let's don't get impatient."

"Listen, Wood, I want to talk to the girl who spotted this hit guy."

He hesitated a moment, then said, "I don't know, Jack—"

"Look, last night you asked me if you could send me a lady. Well, now the answer's yes, and she's the one I want."

"You'll have to pay for her time, Jack," he cautioned me.

"Don't worry about that, Wood, I'll pay her. I'm on my way home now. Have her come to my place at nine, okay?"

"Okay, pal, you got yourself a lady of the evening," he agreed. "You want me to give her any special instructions?"

"Just tell her to make sure the customer is satisfied," I told him.

"Hey, pal, my ladies always satisfy their customers," he told me.

"Yeah, well, this is one customer who's going to let you know if he got his money's worth," I informed him, and hung up.

I was upset with myself for not having talked to the girl myself earlier when Wood had first given me the information. Eddie always told me that there was no information like first-hand information, and I had forgotten that.

I still have a lot to learn about this business, I told myself.

My eyes fell on the bottom drawer of "my" desk, and I reached down and opened it. What was inside was still Eddie's, because I wasn't ready to accept it yet. Eddie had wanted me to qualify with a gun right from the beginning, but after a few trips to the range I decided I didn't like it and I didn't want to continue. If I had to put a hurting on someone, I was confident that I could do it with my hands.

I stared at the .38 in the shoulder holster for a few more minutes, then closed the drawer again.

At least I knew it was there if things got bad enough—only I hoped they'd never get that bad.

Then again, I was investigating a murder, so how much worse could things get?

CHAPTER THIRTY

On the way home from the office I stopped off at the Kentucky Fried Chicken at Times Square for a box of nine pieces, original recipe, with double mashed potatoes, corn on the cob, and a side order of the Colonel's Kentucky fries.

I was finished eating and tucking the remaining four pieces into the refrigerator so I could eat them for breakfast or lunch when there was a knock on my door. I was halfway to the door before I considered that it didn't necessarily have to be Knock Wood Lee's girl who was doing the knocking.

Instead of standing directly in front of the door, I stood off to the side and called out, "Who is it?"

"C'mon, lover, open up," a girl's voice called out. "You've got an eager and anxious lady caller."

It was Tracy Dean.

I opened the door and said, "Hi, Tracy."

"Hi, shamus, want some company?" she asked brightly.

"Uh, I'm expecting—"

"Something smells good," she said, bounding past me. "Smells like the Colonel was here. Do you mind? I'm starved."

I closed the door and told her where she could find the chicken that was left. She took it out, along with a bottle of Miller Lite.

"Want one?" she asked, hoisting the bottle high over her head.

"I've got one started," I told her. Chicken was one of the

127

few things I drank beer with. They just seemed to go together

"What's up, Tracy?" I asked as she seated herself at the table in my kitchenette.

"Can't I come by for a friendly visit without something being up?" she asked, biting into a chicken leg.

Something was wrong. I could count on one hand the times Tracy had been to my place during the year since we'd met. Her coming to me didn't fit the pattern of our relationship.

I sat down opposite her and said, "Don't try to kid me, kid. What's the matter?"

She stared at me over that chicken leg, then lowered it and licked grease from around her lovely mouth.

"I'm depressed," she said finally.

"About what?"

"About my life, where it's going and where it's been."

This could take longer than I had.

"Tracy, I'd like to help, but at the moment I'm expecting someone."

"Oh, who?" she asked.

"Uh, someone who, uh, can help me with a case I'm working on," I stammered. Tracy wasn't a jealous girl, and in fact she had no cause to be. Our relationship didn't warrant it, but I didn't know how she'd feel if she knew I was trying to get her to leave because I was expecting a hooker.

"Confidential, huh?" she asked.

"It's not all that confidential, no, but it is—"

There was a knock at the door just then, and I approached the door the same way I had the first time.

"Jack, what the hell—" Tracy began.

"Just don't move out of that chair for a few minutes, Tracy," I told her. I stood to the side of the door and called out, "Who is it?"

"Knock Wood Lee's friend," a woman's voice called out.

I unlocked the door and let her in.

"Hi, love," she greeted as she walked in. She was a tall black girl, pretty in a slutty sort of way. She had almond-shaped eyes, flaring nostrils and full lips. When she smiled, her teeth were very white. Her body, which was stuffed into a tight blue dress, had taken a lot of stuffing. It was full and firm, full of promise. She wasn't your average Forty-second Street hooker; she was one of Wood's best ladies.

Still, Tracy knew a hooker when she saw one.

I looked at her and found her smiling at me over a piece of chicken.

"I can explain——" I started to tell her.

"A threesome?" the girl asked, removing her short jacket. She dropped it on a chair and walked over to where Tracy was sitting. "I like threesomes," she said, "and your girlfriend's not half bad." She turned to face me and licked her thick lips seductively, saying, "And neither are you."

"What's your name?" I asked her.

"Louise," she answered without hesitation.

That was a refreshing change. Hookers had a habit of picking up nicknames, like "Sweetmeat" or "Polly Pussy" or some such nonsense. Wood didn't go in for that.

"Okay, Louise," I told her, "let's drop the bullshit and get down to business."

She smiled broadly, saying, "Anxious devil, aren't you?" Her hands went behind her to undo her dress, and if Tracy hadn't been there I might have let her get a little farther, just for a quick peek at the merchandise.

"Don't bother undressing," I instructed.

"Oh?" she asked, surprised. "A quickie, with her watching, is that your game?"

I reached into my pocket and came out with five twenties, which I'd tucked in there when I got home. I spread them out like a fan and showed them to her.

"What do I have to do for that?" she asked suspiciously.

"Talk."

Her painted eyebrows went up and she said, "That's all?"

I nodded.

"That's it. I want the name and location of a certain man you spotted a few days ago."

"What man?" she asked, frowning.

"You know what man, Louise. He's the kind of man who kills people for a living. You spotted him the other day and passed on the information. That information found its way to me, but I need more. I need to know who the guy is, where he came from, and where he's staying in New York. For that," I finished, shaking my hundred-dollar fan, "you get this."

"Shit," she said, dropping her hooker act and accent. She grabbed up her jacket again and said, "For that I gets killed, sucker."

I took the jacket from her hand and dropped it back on a chair.

"I can double this, Louise, and guarantee that the man will never know where I got the information," I told her.

She frowned, then asked, "You a cop?"

"No, I'm a fighter."

"Shit, man, I don't go in for no rough stuff," she snapped.

"I don't fight with women, Louise. Look," I explained, "my brother is in jail and my best friend's been murdered. There's a hit man in town, and he may have had something to do with it. I want him, lady. Now, I may not be the cops, but the cops can be brought into it pretty damned quick, and I'd save a couple of hundred bucks. What do you say?"

She kept eyeing the money, but it was the mention of the police that finally made up her mind for her.

"Okay, okay," she said, then licked her lips and said, "the money first."

I gave her the five twenties and said, "Half now and half after you talk."

She took the bills and stuffed them down the front of her dress.

"Okay, I used to work a gig in Detroit, and that's where I recognized this dude from. I never saw him pull a hit, but the circle I traveled in, he was pretty well known for being a mean dude. They called him 'Max the Ax.'"

"What's his M.O.?" I asked.

"Huh?"

"What's he use? An ax or what?"

"Shit, no, he don't use no ax. That was all they could think of to rhyme with his first name."

"What's his full name?"

"Collins, I think. Max Collins. He don't look like a mean dude, but he is. I seen him work a broad over once, and, man, I wanna forget that day."

"Okay, Louise, this is the second hundred-dollar question. Where is he now?"

"Beats the shit outta me, man—and even if you triple that hundred, I couldn't tell you."

I believed her.

"All right then, where did you see him?"

"Fourteenth Street, between First and Second. There's a hotel there; he was in the lobby. I don't know if he's staying there or not, but he was there that day. I was . . . meeting some-one."

"And you don't know what kind of a weapon he uses, or if he even uses one?" I asked.

She shook her head. She didn't know, but that didn't matter. Once I gave Hocus the guy's name, he could check with the Detroit P.D. and get a make on him.

"Okay, Louise, you've earned that extra hundred," I told her. I walked over to my wallet and leafed through the bills in it. I was forty bucks short.

"Um, listen—" I started to say to Louise, but Tracy interrupted. She'd been so quiet the whole time I'd almost forgotten she was there.

"How short are you?" she asked me.

"Forty."

She dug into her little bag and came up with two twenties. I took them, combined them with the mixture of bills I had, and handed them to Louise.

"Thanks, but this ain't gonna do me much good if I gets killed, pal."

"You won't, don't worry."

She picked up her jacket, looking dubious, and then started for the door.

"I'll call Wood and tell him that I'm more than satisfied." I told her.

"Thanks, friend, but next time you need a girl, don't ask for me, okay?"

"Okay."

She started to leave, then turned back and said, "I hope you find your friend's killer, and help your brother, too."

"Thanks."

When she was gone I went over everything she had told me and decided that it had been worth two hundred—uh, one hundred and sixty dollars.

"Thanks for the loan, Tracy," I said, sitting opposite her. "I'll pay you back tomorrow."

"No rush," she told me, cleaning her fingers with a napkin and finishing her bottle of beer.

"Now, you want to tell me why you're so depressed?" I asked.

"Somehow, it doesn't seem so important now," she told me. "I always thought that the fact that you're a private eye was exciting, Jack. Now I see that it can also be scary. Hit men from Detroit? I thought that was only on television."

"They have to come from somewhere, Tracy," I told her.

131

She shook her head, not at what I said but at what she was thinking.

"I came here depressed at the way my life is going, Jack," she told me. "Your friend Eddie is dead, your brother is in jail, and you're about to go looking for a man who kills people for a living." She looked at me and said, "I'm not doing so badly after all, am I?"

I touched her hand and said, "I never thought you were, love."

CHAPTER THIRTY-ONE

When I woke up the next morning I felt a touch of panic.

Eddie's funeral was early that day, and it was in Queens; but what I really wanted to do was go and see Hocus with the info I'd gotten on "Max the Ax."

I also remembered that I was supposed to meet Heck Delgado at ten o'clock to go and see Benny. If I didn't, Benny and maybe even Heck would be disappointed in me. If I missed the funeral, Missy might never speak to me again.

I decided to go to the funeral, for two reasons. One, I wanted to see my best friend off and two, Missy needed someone there with her, and she had no one else but me.

I'd overextended myself with things to do that morning; but Heck and Benny would have to understand, and seeing Hocus would have to wait until later in the day.

What I did, however, was call the Seventeenth Precinct and leave a message for Hocus to meet me in Queens if he possibly could. I added that it would be well worth the trip. I left him the address of both the funeral parlor and the cemetery.

I stayed by Missy the whole time while silent tears rolled down her cheeks. There wasn't much of a turnout, as Eddie hadn't had all that many friends; but there were a few other P.I.'s there who had worked with him over the years, and even some of his old clients showed up.

I didn't know Walker Blue, the P.I. who was working for Heck Delgado, personally, but I knew what he looked like and was surprised to see that he had also attended the services. Eddie knew him, but not all that well. I wished I could go over and talk to him, but I had to stay by Missy. I had a feeling that she would be fine as long as I was right there beside her. I hoped to be able to catch Blue after the ceremony at the cemetery.

Hocus hadn't shown up by the time we were ready to leave the funeral home, and my impatient hope was that he'd make it to the cemetery before we finished there.

As Missy dropped the first handful of dirt on Eddie Waters's coffin to signify the end of the ceremony, Hocus still hadn't arrived.

"Do you want me to come home with you?" I asked Missy, walking her to the limousine.

"No, Jack, there's no need for that. The limo will drop me home. You can catch a ride back to the city with someone here," she told me. "I'll be fine."

"I know you will," I told her, opening the door of the big car for her. "I'll call you later."

She nodded and got into the limo. I shut the door and watched it drive away.

"Mr. Jacoby?" I heard a man's voice call from behind.

I turned to find a tall, gray-haired, distinguished-looking man who I knew was Walker Blue.

Blue was the most flamboyant private investigator in New York City, and possibly in the country. His fees were high, but he consistently delivered what he was paid to. Many of his court appearances as a witness for either side had been well publicized, and he had turned many courtroom procedures into circus events.

The suit Blue was wearing must have cost him more than my entire wardrobe, and his graying hair was neatly trimmed. He had a long-jawed face which was just starting to show the wear of his age, which had to be over fifty. Eddie had always said that Walker Blue looked like a Fancy Dan, but when it came to getting down and dirty, he was a mean mother.

"Mr. Jacoby, my name is Walker Blue," he said, extending his hand. I accepted it and we shook hands somberly.

"Hector has explained the situation as regards your involvement in this case," he explained, "and I can't say that I agree with him. However, I will not attempt to argue the point. I only wish to inform you that I work alone and I consult with no one. When I have results, I will report them to Hector. It will not be necessary for you and me to have any contact whatsoever about this case. If you should come across some information you think is noteworthy, you can give it to Hector and he will add it to mine."

I was at a loss as to how to react to the man and his speech. I had been willing to work with him, and he had made it perfectly clear that he was not willing to work with me.

Well, then fuck him.

"I'm sorry about your friend," he told me, "and it was good to meet you. I'm afraid I have to be going." With that he turned on his heels and walked away.

"You could have fooled me," I said to his retreating back, but if he heard me at all he chose to ignore the remark.

"He's a little hard to take," a voice said from behind me. I turned and found Detective Hocus standing there looking at Walker Blue's back.

"You've dealt with him?" I asked.

He nodded.

"Once or twice. His attitude is shitty, but there's no denying he's a brilliant investigator," he commented.

"Yeah, well, he's got a lot to learn about being a human being," I told him.

"I agree. You need a ride to the city?" he asked.

"Yeah, I do, thanks."

We walked to his car, and I waited until we were on the L.I.E. heading for the city before I brought up the subject of "Max the Ax."

"Ever hear of a hit man called Max the Ax?" I asked.

"What's his last name?" he asked.

"Collins."

He thought a moment, then shook his head.

"No, can't say that I have. Where's he work out of?"

"Detroit."

"Well, we can check it easily enough. Is this info reliable?" he asked.

"I believe so, yes."

"All right. When I get back to the precinct I'll send off a message to the Detroit P.D. and see what they have on Max the Ax. Jesus, what a name!"

"What does this mean to you?" I asked him.

He glanced over at me.

"Honestly?"

135

"I wouldn't have asked if I didn't want an honest answer," I told him.

"It doesn't mean a hell of a lot."

"Doesn't it raise a question?" I asked.

"It sure does. It raises the question of who this guy is here to hit."

"You don't think he's made his hit yet?"

"If he had, Jacoby, he wouldn't still be here," he told me.

The answer made too much sense for me to like it; but it was honest, and that was what I had asked for.

CHAPTER THIRTY-TWO

I had Hocus drop me off as soon as we came out of the Midtown Tunnel, with intentions of walking over to the hotel where Louise told me she had spotted Max the Ax.

I was halfway to Fourteenth Street when I realized that I had not gotten a physical description of the Detroit hit man from her. I had simply never thought to ask.

I thought about what Hocus had said about Walker Blue being a brilliant investigator. What would Hocus, or Blue, have said about my standing there in the street with egg on my face? What was I going to do, ask the desk clerk if a hit man from Detroit was registered there, and by the way, could he point him out to me?

I found a pay phone and dialed Knock Wood Lee's phone number. When Tiger answered I asked for him, and she told me he wasn't there.

"Maybe you can help me, Lee."

"I'd love to try," she teased.

"I need a location for a hooker called Louise. I need to talk to her again."

"Didn't you see her last night?" she asked, sounding puzzled. "Wood won't like it if she stood you up—"

"No, no, it's nothing like that. She showed last night, but there was something I forgot to ask her. If you could just tell me where she's working—"

"She wouldn't be out this early, Jack. She'd still be home, probably asleep."

"Sweetheart, I hate to ask this, but could you let me have her address? Or her phone number?"

"The phone wouldn't do any good," she told me. "She unplugs it when she goes to sleep."

She went silent, and I knew she was thinking over my request, so I gave her all the time she needed.

"Does this have to do with Eddie Waters," she asked, "and your brother?"

It might, I thought, but I said, "Yes, it does."

"Okay, Jack, she's got an apartment over on West Twelfth at Eighth Avenue, above the bookstore. Don't tell Wood, okay?"

"You're a doll. I'll wait a week and then call Wood and ask for your hand in marriage."

"I'll hold my breath."

I hung up, knowing full well that I wouldn't have to tell Wood, because she'd do that herself.

I hoofed it over to Eighth Avenue and Twelfth Street and easily found the bookstore Lee was talking about. It was done up in red neon against a black background, with a sign in the window that glowed: Foul Play. It was a bookstore that dealt exclusively in mystery books.

Very appropriate, I remember thinking, not realizing how appropriate it really was.

I found the door to the second floor unlocked, and inside there were two mailboxes. One was empty, and the other had a couple of envelopes in it, so I figured I'd try that one first. The mailbox with the envelopes in it had a large *F* pasted on it, so I assumed that meant "front."

I started up the creaking stairway, trying to ignore the stench of stale urine, and knocked on the first door. When there was no answer I experienced a strong feeling of déjà vu. I stepped aside before knocking again, harder this time, but there was still no answer.

Wrong apartment, I told myself, try the other one; but I reached down for the knob and it turned freely.

I didn't want to go in, because I was afraid of what I was going to find. I stood there in the hall for a few minutes, my heart pounding, just staring at the door as it stood a couple of inches ajar. Finally I took a deep, shuddering breath and pushed the door open.

There was blood everywhere, and I took two quick steps to my left and threw up. Not having eaten that morning, it was mostly painful dry heaving, with a touch of green bile thrown in for color. When it subsided I steeled myself and looked again.

There was a bed in the center of the room, and Louise was lying on it face up. Blood stained the ceiling and the sheets, and her eyes were wide open and staring with a puzzled look in them, as if she were trying to figure out who the hell had bled all over her ceiling.

I walked into the room and got just close enough to see the large, gaping wound in her throat. It looked like it might have even been done with an . . .

Jesus Christ!

It looked like it could very well have been done with an ax!

CHAPTER THIRTY-THREE

I called Hocus direct, preferring not to fuck around with a 911 phone call.

"What am I, Jacoby, your favorite cop?" he asked in a tired voice.

I told him if he only had dimples I'd marry him, and could he hurry up and get his ass over here. He said he'd be there in fifteen minutes.

When he arrived I was sitting out in the hall on the floor, on the other side of the door from my puddle of bile. He looked at me and then at the puddle and then back at me.

"So I'm not so hardboiled," I told him, shrugging my shoulders. "She's in there."

"M.E.'s right behind me," he said, and walked into the room. "Jesus!" I heard him breathe.

Dr. Mahbee, the M.E., came up next and repeated Hocus's performance.

"In there," I said, flicking my thumb.

He went in, and I didn't hear any audible reaction from him; but then blood was his business, wasn't it?

As the rest of the troops arrived I directed them all to the proper room from my seated position on the floor. I didn't have the strength in my legs that was needed to stand up.

Wright, Hocus's partner, was the last one up, and when he walked in he reacted the same way his partner had.

I became aware that there was some arguing going on inside

the room, but I couldn't make out what it was all about. A few minutes later Hocus came storming out, breathing fire. He stepped over me, then joined me in sitting on the floor.

"What's the beef?" I asked him.

"That asshole captain in there wants me to put the cuffs on you."

"On me? What the fuck—is finding bodies against the law now?" I asked. "Jesus, at least I report the damned things!"

"Jacoby, you have kind of been getting involved with one or two too many these past few days. I mean, you personally found two, and you're involved with two others."

"So here," I said, extending my wrists, "I'll make it easy for you."

"Don't be stupid," he said, again sounding tired, even more so than he had on the phone. "This is a Homicide investigation, and I'm in charge, not that asshole in blue."

"Oh."

We sat in silence for a while, and I finally broke it by saying, "Jesus, this is starting to scare the shit out of me."

"I don't blame you. Somebody sure sawed that broad wide open. Who was she?"

I explained who she was and why I had come to see her.

"Max the Ax," he said.

"What's the M.E. say?" I asked.

"I don't know. We'll ask him when he comes out."

"What's with this captain?"

"He's a stickler for department policy, a by-the-book jerk," he commented.

At that moment Mahbee came out, looked around, then looked down and stared at the both of us sitting on our rumps on the dirty floor. He seemed to consider something, then he shrugged, stepped over both of us and joined us on the floor.

"What's the verdict, Doc?" Hocus asked, seated in the middle.

"Something cleaved her open good," the East Indian replied.

"An ax?" I asked, the words catching in my throat.

He looked at me kind of puzzled, then nodded slightly and said, "No, I don't believe so, although I can see where you might think so."

"What then?" Hocus asked.

"A sharp knife and a strong man," he replied. "The cut went from right to left," he said, illustrating with a swipe at the air, "indicating the possibility that the killer was left-handed. You

142

tend to slice across your body," he told us, demonstrating by whipping his right hand from left to right, with his thumb extended, as if braced against the back of a blade.

"No ax," I said quietly.

"Looks like an ax," Hocus commented.

"I could see where you might think so," Mahbee said again.

I looked at Hocus and he looked at me.

"Maybe that's where the name came from," I suggested.

He nodded, saying, "We don't have anything back from Detroit yet—or at least, we didn't when I left. Maybe when I get back we'll find out."

At that point the captain came walking out, and when he saw the three of us seated on the floor in the hall—well, it must have offended his by-the-book sensibilities. If looks could kill he would have had three more corpses right there in the hall.

"I'm conducting an investigation, Cap," Hocus told him. The captain was a short, pale-skinned, red-haired man, and he compressed his lips until they turned white, then turned on his heels and stalked down the steps.

Dr. Mahbee's men came out of the room next, with the body all wrapped up and ready to go.

Struggling to his feet, Mahbee told Hocus, "I'll let you know more after I do an autopsy."

As he started to leave I remembered something and almost jumped out of my skin calling after him.

"Doctor!"

"Yes?"

"Ah, the body from the Roger Williams Hotel—" I began.

"Purcell?" he asked.

"That's the one. What was the cause of death on him?"

He looked at Hocus first, who probably nodded his head, and then told me, "His heart, it simply failed, apparently while he was being tortured."

"Then you wouldn't say he was deliberately murdered?"

He shook his head.

"I would say that someone was attempting to get some information from him, and he simply died on them."

"Okay, thanks."

He nodded to both of us and followed his men down the steps.

"I meant to tell you that," Hocus told me, "but we got involved."

"That's okay," I assured him.

"You were wondering if Purcell might not have been on Max's hit list?" he asked.

"It was a thought."

"I guess."

"Here's another one."

"What?"

"If Max the Ax had nothing to do with Corky Purcell's death, then who the fuck were the two guys I ran into at his hotel room?"

He shrugged and replied, "Just a couple more loose ends."

CHAPTER THIRTY-FOUR

Hocus and his partner went back to the precinct to check the Teletype messages for an answer from Detroit. I went to Packy's for a few quick beers, then used his phone to call Heck Delgado. I wanted to make sure he understood the reason I hadn't been able to meet him that morning.

After I'd explained he told me, "I understand, Miles, but you'll have to explain it to your brother. He thinks you've abandoned him."

"That's just fucking stupid," I told him, getting angry at my brother. "Didn't you tell him that I was working for you? Shit, the cops are starting to look at me funny because I'm turning up so many goddamned stiffs. Some asshole captain wanted to lock me up today for reporting another body."

"Another body?" he asked, puzzled. "You mean, aside from the one you found in the hotel?"

"Yeah," I told him, then explained how and why I had discovered the dead hooker in her apartment.

"You think this hit man from Detroit killed her because he knew she had spotted him?" he asked.

"Well, I don't see talent being imported to kill some small-time whore, so I guess that's the only premise that fits the situation," I agreed.

"Will you want to come with me the next time I see your brother, Miles?"

"Will they let me in anytime I want, Heck?"

"Let me know when you want to go and I'll arrange it."

"Ah, make it tomorrow, will you? I might as well get it over with."

To Heck's credit he ignored the tone of my voice and said, "I'll arrange it, Miles. Let me know what you find out about this hit man, will you?"

"Sure."

I hung up and kept my hand on the receiver, picked it up again and dialed Julie's number.

"Hello?" she answered, her voice sounding as if I had just awakened her.

"Julie, it's Miles."

There was a brief pause, and then she said, "Hello, Miles."

I hadn't thought it would be that awkward, but then what could I expect?

"How are you?"

"I'm fine, Miles. How are you?"

"I'm fine," I told her.

There was more silence, and I was just about ready to hang up when she said, "Oh, Miles, this is just silly. There's no reason for us to be this awkward with each other."

"I agree," I said.

"Come on over and I'll fix us some lunch," she told me. "I've just been moping around here, anyway."

"Okay, that sounds good," I said, "even if it's just to give you something to do."

"That's not what I meant, you boob," she scolded me. "I want to see you."

"I want to see you, too," I told her, then added quickly, "maybe you'll even let me bounce some theories off of you."

"Sure, if it'll help. I'll be your assistant detective."

"Never mind being assistant detective, just have a decent lunch ready. Suddenly I'm starving."

This may have been just what I needed, to have somebody to use as a sounding board, to talk it all out, and at the same time dispose of any awkwardness we might feel toward each other over what had happened the other night.

"You look like somebody just gave you a split decision," Packy said when I gave him back his phone.

"That's the way I feel, Pack. I'll see you later."

"How's Benny?"

I looked at him and then said, "I don't know, I haven't seen him."

146

He looked back at me strangely and I got up and left.

I hoofed it over to Julie and Benny's apartment. She answered the door wearing her usual outfit of old jeans and equally old sweatshirt. She had never looked better. The sweatshirt was one of a few that Benny had made up when I started fighting. It said Kid Jacoby across the front in bright red letters.

"Where'd you get that?" I asked her.

"Benny has a few left," she told me. "I wear them around the house when I don't care what I look like.

I bit back a remark about how good she looked and asked what was for lunch instead.

"I thought I'd just cook up some burgers and fries, if that's okay with you," she told me.

"That's fine."

"Come on into the kitchen," she said. "We can talk while I cook."

I watched as she moved around the kitchen, admiring the way her breasts moved underneath the sweatshirt. I couldn't help thinking that if Benny should be found guilty, he'd be put away for a long time. He couldn't really expect Julie to wait for him.

But he wasn't guilty. He couldn't have killed Eddie.

"What was it you wanted to talk about?" she asked, breaking into my thoughts.

"Well, basically I just wanted to be able to talk out loud to someone, just to review the case for myself."

"Well, go ahead," she told me. "I can cook and listen at the same time."

I started talking, recapping the case: Benny was admittedly drunk and had also admitted going to see Eddie to argue about my getting my license. Missy said that after Benny went into Eddie's office, she heard what sounded like a fight. She got scared and called for the police. When the police arrived, they found Eddie dead and subsequently found Benny wandering around the building, apparently looking for a way out.

"It doesn't sound good, does it?" she asked.

"No. From the time that Missy ran downstairs to wait for the cops to the time that they found Eddie's body, Benny had to have left the office, someone else had to have come in and beaten Eddie to death, and then split."

"Was there enough time for that?" she asked.

"There has to have been," I answered.

She knew what I meant and nodded. If we admitted that

there wasn't enough time, then we admitted that Benny probably did kill Eddie.

"Now, I've been checking some of Eddie's dissatisfied clients and so has Missy, and neither one of us can come up with anyone who had any reason to want him dead. Somebody's afraid we'll find something out, though, because—"

"Because what?" she asked.

I had stopped short because I was about to tell her that someone had sent three jerks after me to work me over, which I hadn't previously mentioned to her.

"Uh, because—"

She turned away from the stove and put her hands on her hips.

"If you're going to talk it out, Miles, you'd be better off not leaving anything out," she told me.

She was right, so I went ahead and kept talking, telling her how I got knocked on the head and then did some damage myself.

"I thought you were taking longer to heal than you normally do," she observed.

She brought the burgers and fries to the table and sat across from me.

"So then it has to be one of his clients," she decided. "Someone who you talked to."

"Maybe."

"Who else could it be?" she asked.

That was when I told her about Max the Ax and about the bodies I kept finding.

"What has this man Purcell to do with Benny's case?" she asked.

"Nothing, really," I told her. I then explained why I had gone to visit Purcell, looking for information on the man in the fifth row.

Then I told her about Louise and finding her dead in her apartment.

"Oh, that must have been horrible," she said.

"It wasn't pretty. The police and I figure that Max did her in because he knew she'd recognized him."

"Do the police think that maybe this man from Detroit killed Eddie?" she asked.

"I'm afraid not," I said, picking up the last of the fries. "They feel that if the Ax had already made his hit, he wouldn't still be in town."

148

"Who says he's still in town?" she asked.

"That's what I'm going to find out," I told her, "as soon as Detective Hocus comes up with a pedigree on him."

"Pedigree?"

"A history and description. I've got to know what he looks like before I can go looking for him."

She was silent for a few seconds, then she touched my arm and said, "Miles, when you find him—"

"Yeah?"

"Well, when you find him, what if he kills you?"

"I've tried not to think about that," I told her.

"I wouldn't want to lose both Benny and you, Miles. That would be more than I could stand."

I put my hand on hers and said, "Nobody says you're going to lose either one of us, Julie. Not if I have something to say about it," I added, sounding ridiculously macho even to myself.

"What if the hit man was here to kill this Purcell man," she asked, "and has nothing at all to do with Eddie Waters?"

"Then I'm barking up the wrong tree," I told her. Then a thought struck me and must have been reflected on my face.

"What?" she asked.

"If Max the Ax killed Corky Purcell," I told her, "then that means he must be after the man in the fifth row, too." I stood up, starting to get excited. "Sure, that's got to be it. What else could they have wanted to know from Purcell that was worth torturing him for? One of the men who ran into me must have been the Ax."

"And the other one?"

"I don't know—an extra hand, maybe. Maybe the other one located Purcell and then called the Ax in. Now, if Purcell died of a heart attack before he could tell them where to find the guy from the fifth row, that means that the Ax must still be in town."

"It sounds like it makes sense," she said, then added, "but none of that helps Benny, does it?"

She hit home with that and I sat back down, feeling deflated.

"No, I guess it doesn't."

"Miles, do you suppose he could have done it?"

"What?" I asked in surprise.

"Do you suppose that Benny could have been that drunk and angry that he could have—"

"Julie, no—I, uh, no, it couldn't be. Don't even think it," I told her.

149

"All right, Miles," she said, rising and beginning to clean the table.

I stood up and said, "Julie, I've got to go and check in with Hocus, see if he came up with anything on the Ax. Thanks for the lunch, though, and for letting me talk at you."

"That's okay, Miles. I'm glad you came over."

"Yeah, so am I."

"Let me know what's happening, okay?"

"Sure."

She walked me to the door, then said, "Miles, how is Eddie's secretary?"

Julie had never met either Eddie or Missy, but that was the kind of person she was, concerned about Missy's feelings.

"She's all right," I said, "considering she was more than just his secretary. We buried him this morning."

She touched my arm and said, "I'm sorry. I know you were great friends."

"Yeah—well, I've got to go. I'll call you."

"Okay. Be careful, Miles."

"Don't worry," I assured her, "that's one of my prime concerns."

CHAPTER THIRTY-FIVE

"There's his sheet," Hocus said, flipping it across his desk at me, "you can read it if you want, but I can give it to you in a nutshell."

"Go ahead," I said, scanning the Teletype sheet but listening at the same time.

"Max uses a knife," he told me, "but he got his name because he's so strong, and keeps his blade so sharp, that his victims often look as if they've been cleaved with an ax."

"He take any falls?" I asked.

"One, but he was just a kid. He took an assault-one rap and served his time."

"Is he hot in Detroit?"

"Nope. The word we get is that he works out of Detroit, but he never shits where he lives."

"Got a description?" I asked, but then I located it myself on the sheet. "Five nine, one seventy, light-brown hair, early thirties. Reads like a college boy, not a killer," I commented.

"He's a mean mother, Jacoby. I wouldn't advise crossing his trail if I were you. He may not look it, but he's as mean as they come—or so they tell me."

"What are you going to do now?" I asked, sailing the sheet back at him.

"We'll keep an eye out for him," he told me, picking up the sheet.

"That's it?"

"What do you want me to do, transmit a felony alarm on him?" he asked. "Where's my justification? So somebody saw him in town, so what? There's a lot of people in town."

"Yeah, but how many of them kill people with a knife, almost cutting their heads off? What about the dead hooker?"

"What about her? I've got some people working the area. We come up with a description that matches Maxie, and then maybe I can transmit some kind of alarm. Right now, I got nothing on him except that he may be in town, and that sure as hell ain't illegal—yet."

"Yeah, okay," I said, getting to my feet, "so your hands are tied, but mine aren't."

He stood up and pointed a warning finger at me.

"Jacoby, you tangle with this dude and you'll be getting in way over your head. I'm warning you, he's out of your league."

What could I say to that? The man couldn't have been righter, but I wasn't about to admit that to him.

"We'll see," I shot back lamely.

"I got enough stiffs, Jacoby," he told me, "I don't need any more. And not everybody is as conscientious about reporting bodies as you are. You're liable to lie where you die for days before we find you."

"Jesus Christ," I said to nobody in particular, "a poetic cop."

"Get out of here," he snapped, sitting back down, "I got enough wisecracks, too, without having to listen to yours. Keep your ass out of trouble, that's all I ask."

"I appreciate the concern," I told him. "If I turn up anything I think you can use, I'll let you know."

"God save me from rookies," he said to my retreating back.

Out on the street I realized that he was right. I was virtually a rookie in the private-eye biz, but this was one rookie who was going to get some experience pretty damned quick, and would learn by it.

If I managed to stay alive, that is.

152

CHAPTER THIRTY-SIX

I found myself heading for the office without consciously intending to. When I stopped to think about it I knew what I was going there for, and it scared me.

Both Julie and Hocus had indicated that they didn't think I could handle a hit man from Detroit. Up until recently the only hit man from Detroit I would have thought I had to worry about was Thomas Hearns, but this was the real thing.

When I got to the office I used my key to open the door and then reached in to turn on the light before entering. When I was satisfied that everything was as it should be, I crossed the room to the door leading to the inner office. I repeated the procedure, reaching in and turning on the light, then checking the room out from the doorway before entering. Once I was satisfied that all was well, I relaxed considerably.

I walked to "my" desk and seated myself behind it.

If I was going to go up against a professional blade man, I had to be one up on him. I opened the bottom drawer of the desk where Eddie kept the .38 and stared at it. Although I was familiar with it from those earlier sessions at the range, when Eddie had first tried to get me to qualify with it, I wasn't a professional marksman by any means, but Max the Ax had to get close to me if he was going to use his blade, and at that range I wouldn't be likely to miss.

I hoped.

I took the gun and holster out of the drawer and opened the gun to check the cylinder. It was loaded with five shots, with an empty chamber under the hammer. I reached further back in the drawer and came up with a box of shells and a clip-on belt holster. I dropped a few extra shells in my pocket, then put the box and the shoulder rig back and shut the drawer. Standing up, I clipped the holster onto my belt in back and slid the .38 home. It wasn't very comfortable, but the thought that the gun might save my life made it bearable. As I shut the desk lamp the phone rang, making me jump a good foot. I stared at it for two more rings, then picked it up.

"Private investigator," I said.

"I hear you're looking for me," a man's voice said.

"That depends," I told him. "Who are you?"

"I'm the man who thinks you should stay away from south-paws, Kid."

"You're Corky Purcell's friend?" I asked him.

"Yeah," he muttered, "poor Corky. He loaned me his ticket and got killed for it."

"Look, I've been wanting to thank you," I told him, "but now I think you're in trouble. There's a man in town—"

"I know about him," he told me. "You'd stay healthier if you'd forget about me," he suggested. "I'll accept your thanks—"

"And my help, I hope," I cut in, "because I'm still offering it."

"Well, as long as you know what you're getting into," he said.

"I'm prepared for the worst," I said, touching the .38.

"I guess that's it then. I do need help. I'm not fool enough to think I can avoid this guy forever."

"Where can we meet?" I asked him.

"Let me think," he said, and he took so long I thought maybe he'd hung up. "Okay, meet me under the West Side Highway, at Fifty-fifth Street, in an hour."

"Okay, it's a date."

"Uh, listen, thanks, Kid."

"Yeah, sure, friend. I owe you one, anyway."

He hung up before I had a chance to ask him for his name.

I started to leave the office, and then thought better of it. If I went to meet this guy without letting someone know about it and something happened, it might be days before they found my body. I called the only person I could trust.

"Julie, listen," I told her when she answered, and then explained that I was meeting someone and told her where. That was all I told her. "If I don't call you in, say, two hours, call Hocus and tell him where I went. You got that?"

"Yes, Miles, but—"

"Just do this for me, okay?"

"All right, Miles—but be careful."

I promised I would and hung up.

As I left the office I felt for the gun on my back, making sure it fit snugly into the holster. The weight of it was comforting as I rode down in the elevator.

I just hoped a cop didn't catch me with it.

CHAPTER THIRTY-SEVEN

"You don't look like one of them fags what likes to meet under the highway, you know?" the cab driver told me as he turned down Fifty-fifth Street.

"What do I look like?" I asked him, squirming in the backseat because the gun butt was digging into my back.

"You look more like a pug with your mug kind of busted up like that," he observed. "I used to do some fighting myself when I was younger."

"Is that a fact?" I asked.

"Yeah—here we are, Mac. Fifty-fifth and the West Side Highway. If we had some more time I'd tell you about some of my big fights."

"Maybe next time," I said, paying the fare and tipping him generously.

"Hey, thanks, Mac," he said, taking the money. He looked closer at me and said, "Naw, you ain't a fag. Hope you didn't take no offense."

"None at all," I assured him. "Thanks for the ride."

"Anytime, Mac."

He made a left turn on Twelfth and drove back down Fifty-fourth.

I turned and peered under the highway. The sun had just gone down and there was still some daylight left, but under the highway it was black as night.

"Shit," I said to myself. In a few moments it would be just as dark everywhere else, and then I'd be a sitting duck.

Now why the hell did I think of that now?

It didn't do my nerves any good, either.

Underneath the highway were parked cars, abandoned cars, debris from vandalized cars and from the highway itself, which was on the verge of collapse.

Somewhere in among all of that junk was either a frightened ex-trainer, or a brutal hit man.

Jesus, my hands were shaking and my knees were weak. It wasn't love, so I knew I must be scared shitless.

It was getting darker by the second, and I was getting fidgety waiting for someone to make their presence known. If the man from the fifth row was already there . . . somewhere . . . he must have been able to tell by then that I had come alone.

Three different times I started to reach for the gun and then stopped myself. If my man was in there somewhere, the sight of a gun wouldn't comfort him any. Then again, he was waiting so damned long to show himself that he wasn't doing much for my comfort.

I finally got tired of waiting and decided to either leave or go under the highway after him.

The whole trip would have been worth shit if I left, so I went under the highway after him.

"Hello," I called out.

The only answer I got was a slight echo.

It was colder underneath the highway, as if I were standing in a wind tunnel. I kidded myself that the chill that I felt was solely a product of that cold.

"Hello," I called out again, still with no response.

I'd just about had enough and was ready to call it a bad meet when a thought hit me that maybe my man was there and *unable* to answer.

Maybe he was dead.

The chill I felt worsened as I decided to check inside some of the cars, hoping I wouldn't find another body. Hocus might not be able to keep from putting the cuffs on me next time.

Instead of checking the parked cars, which would almost definitely be locked, I started to check some of the vandalized and burnt-out wrecks.

As I opened the door of one of them and prepared to stick my head in, I caught a movement from the backseat out of the corner of my eye and jerked my head away just in time to keep my throat from being cut.

"Oh, shit!" I shouted as I felt the tip tear at my throat. I felt the warmth of my own blood as it seemed to pour down over my chest. In my mind's eye I could see that my throat was slashed wide open, as if it had been cloven with an ax; but that was obviously just in my mind, because I was still alive.

As I pulled back and away from the car I got my feet tangled and fell to the ground, putting myself in a very vulnerable position. Luckily my assailant had to get out of the backseat of the car by climbing over the front seat and was not able to take immediate advantage. I scrambled away from the car, scraping my hands and knees in the process. I was trying to regain my feet while also attempting to pull the gun from behind my back. I had almost gotten to my feet when I tripped over a large chunk of debris and went sprawling again.

Panic threatened to blind me, but I kept my head and kept rolling, trying to stay out of range of that deadly blade until I could get back to my feet and get the gun out.

He was out of the car by this time and advancing on me, just a shadowy figure whose face I couldn't see.

The gun seemed to catch on the back of my jacket, and I tried to counteract that problem by yelling, "I've got a gun, I've got a gun!"

Hearing him laugh didn't help my confidence any. I just about had the gun loose when I felt his foot catch me in my left side, sending me to the ground again. I used my hands to break my fall, managing to hold onto the gun somehow. I turned in time to see the shadow of his arm and the gleam of the knife as he swung it at me, and I felt the tip cut through my jacket and shirt and rip through the flesh of my side.

As I flinched in pain I accidently squeezed off a shot from the .38.

After that I could have sworn that the entire West Side Highway fell in on my head.

CHAPTER THIRTY-EIGHT

No one could have been more surprised than I was when I woke up, because I would have called it a safe bet that I was dead.

The only reason I could think of to explain the fact that I was still alive was that Collins must have thought I was bluffing about having a gun, and when I squeezed off a round accidentally he must have then realized that I wasn't and taken off.

Luckily, he hadn't left me dead, but he did leave me cut up some. My chest was slick with the blood from my throat wound, and I could feel my shirt sticking to the wound on my right side. I didn't know how much blood I had lost, but I was feeling very weak. Getting to my feet took a major effort on my part, and I didn't think I could get very much further than that on my own.

Across the street from where I was there was a phone booth, and I set my mind on making it at least that far. I stumbled a few times—once slipping on a patch of my own blood, which is always a thrill—but finally made it to the booth, which was one of the older kind. It actually *was* a booth, but the door was missing and the light didn't work. I could forgive it for that, however, as long as the phone worked.

I stuffed myself into the booth and grabbed the headset off the hook. The buzzing sound it made in my ear was one of the most welcome sounds I'd ever heard.

Having established that the phone worked, I set about trying to find a dime, but came up empty. To my credit—take a bow, Jacoby—I did not panic. You do not need a dime to dial the operator, so that's what I did.

"Operator," a dehumanized famale voice promptly answered.

"Op—" I started to say, but that was as far as I got. It was the first time I'd tried to speak since waking up, and the words stuck in my throat. My neck was tremendously sore from the knife wound, and I tried to clear my throat so I could speak clearly.

"Hello?" the voice asked. "This is the Operator. Can I help you?"

"Yes," I was finally able to rasp. "Operator, I'm in a, uh, pay phone and I don't have a dime. I'd like to—to make a call and charge it to—to my home number," I told her haltingly.

"Hold on, please," she told me. A couple of clicks later another female voice came on and asked me if she could help me. I cleared my throat and went through my request again.

"What is your number, sir?" she asked.

I gave it to her, and then she asked me a hard one: What number did I want to call?

I hadn't thought about that.

What number did I want to call?

"What number do you want to call, sir?" she asked me again.

"Uh—" I said, just to let her know I was still there while I frantically searched my brain for a number.

I finally gave her the only one I could think of.

"I'll connect you, sir. You will be billed at your home number. Have a nice evening."

The phone rang twice and then was answered.

"Hello?"

It was Julie, and I hadn't even realized that it was her number I'd given.

"Hello?" she said again.

"Julie," I finally managed to say, hoping I didn't sound too much like a frog, or an obscene caller.

"Jack, is that you? I've been frantic! You didn't give me a chance to say anything when you called—are you all right?"

"I need a little help, Julie," I told her.

"What happened? Are you all right?" she asked again.

162

"I need to be picked up. Can you get a cab and pick me up?" I asked her.

"Jack, what happened, for God's sake—"

"Don't ask any questions now, Julie, please. Can you do it?"

"I can—yes, I can borrow a car, my girlfriend's car, but—"

"Do that, then," I said. "We won't have to deal with a cab driver. And bring a blanket."

"A blanket? What for?"

"Julie, honey, just get over here. I'm on Fifty-fifth Street, by the West Side Highway. Spread the blanket on the backseat. I'm, uh, I'm losing some blood—"

"Blood? Oh Jack, I was afraid of something like this—" she hesitated, not saying anything more but sounding as if my getting hurt was something she had expected all along.

"Julie, I really need you over here as soon as possible," I told her urgently.

"I'm on my way, darling," she said, and hung up.

I didn't even have the strength to hang up the phone. I just let it go and slid to the floor of the booth to wait for her to come. I sincerely hoped she'd arrive before I bled to death.

I must have passed out, or dozed off, because I didn't even know she was there until she was shaking me with both hands, trying to wake me up.

"Jack!" she was shouting, shaking me violently. "Jack, wake up!"

"Julie?" I asked, squinting my eyes at her until her face came into focus.

"Oh, thank God!" she breathed. "I thought you were dead." It was then that she noticed that her hands were sticky with my blood. "Oh, God," she said quietly. She wiped her hands on her pants and said, "C'mon, we've got to get you in the car and to a hospital."

A hospital, I thought, and she literally dragged me to my feet and stuffed me into the backseat of the borrowed car.

Jesus, why the hell hadn't I thought to call an ambulance or the cops, for Christ's sake, instead of calling her and alarming her?

Why was her number the only number I could think of when I was in trouble?

CHAPTER THIRTY-NINE

It wasn't until we were inside the hospital, underneath the bright lights, that Julie saw just how much blood I was covered with.

Hell, *I* didn't even know how much blood I had been covered with. Between the wound to my throat and the one on my side, I was almost covered with red stains from head to toe.

"Jesus, Jack!" she whispered as we entered the emergency room.

"It's not as bad as it looks," I told her.

"Christ, I hope not."

When we finally got a doctor to come out and take me into an examining room, Julie said, "I'll wait right here."

"I'll be out soon," I assured her.

The doctor stretched me out on an examining table and began to remove my shirt.

"Ouch," I said as he pulled the shirt away from my side wound.

"How did this happen?" he asked.

I explained that I had been the victim of an attempted mugging, and had been cut when I tried to fight.

"Your money's not worth your life," he told me wisely.

"I guess not."

While he sewed me up I had nothing to look at but his face. He was about fifty or so, with dark bushy eyebrows and a mustache to match. His hands had an antiseptic smell that was making me feel sick.

"Your throat isn't too bad," he told me. "It just bled a lot. It's stopped by itself."

It was my side that needed sewing up, and as he was finishing he said, "This took about twenty stitches. You should stay in the hospital overnight, but that's up to you."

"I'd rather go home to bed," I told him.

"As long as you stay there. You do too much moving around and you're going to bust these stitches wide open."

I promised him I'd stay in bed.

"I'll have to file a report with the police," he told me as he helped me sit up.

"That's fine with me," I told him. "I'll be making a report of my own in the morning, anyway."

I got down from the table and started pulling on the tattered remains of my blood-soaked shirt.

"Thanks, Doc," I told him.

"That's okay. Just don't ruin my work by breaking open those stitches. Leave your name and address at the desk."

"Sure."

When I walked out Julie ran to my side and grabbed my arm.

"Are you all right?" she asked.

"Yeah, I took some stitches, but I'm okay."

"C'mon, let's go," she told me, heading for the door.

"What about paying?"

"I took care of it," she told me.

Outside the hospital I slid into the passenger seat next to her as she started the car.

"Jesus Christ!" I snapped when I realized that the gun and holster were no longer clipped to the back of my belt. "Oh, shit!" I added, for good measure.

"What's wrong, Jack?" she asked.

"We have to go back," I told her.

"Back where? To the hospital?"

I thought about it.

"No, not the hospital," I decided. If I'd had it at the hospital, the doctor would have made some remark.

"Then where?"

"The phone booth," I told her. "We've got to go back to the phone booth."

"What for?"

166

"I lost something."

"Something important?" she asked. "You shouldn't be on your feet."

"I won't be," I told her. "I promise—if we find what I lost, I'll go right home to bed."

Shaking her head she said, "All right."

She drove us back to the phone booth on Fifty-fifth Street, by the West Side Highway.

"I'll get out and look," she said, starting to open her door.

"No!" I snapped, then when she looked shocked I said in a softer tone, "I'll go and look myself. I know what I'm looking for."

I opened the door on my side and gingerly stepped out of the car.

"Don't bend over," she shouted after me.

I walked over to the phone booth, but it was so dark inside that I couldn't see the floor.

"Open that door again," I told her, indicating the door on the passenger side which I had closed behind me. She leaned over and opened it, pushing it wide, and the light from inside the car fell on the floor of the phone booth.

There the little beggar was, all snug and covered with blood. I did a fancy, deep knee bend, one hand on my side and the other stretching out for the gun.

"Jesus!" I said as I felt a pain in my side, but my fingers touched the gun and I pulled it toward me.

"Did you find it?" she called from the car.

I turned to face her, clipping the holster to the back of my belt at the same time.

"Yes," I answered, sliding into the car next to her, "I found it."

"What was—".

"What do you say we pick up something to eat?" I asked.

"Are you sure you can eat?" she asked. "I mean, with your throat like that?"

I touched the bandage on my throat, then said, "I could force down some junk food."

She shot me a wry look, then started the motor and said, "I'll settle for Chinese."

That's what we did. We stopped off at a Chinese restaurant, and while I waited in the car she went in to get it.

"My place," I told her when she came back and got behind the wheel.

"Nope," she said, "my place."

"My place is clean," I argued, "I promise. No clothing all over the—"

"We haven't talked about this yet, because you don't want to scare me," she told me, making my concern about scaring her sound ridiculous, "but someone obviously tried to kill you tonight. They can always find you at your place, Jack," she pointed out, "but not at mine."

She had a point.

"Okay, so you're a smart broad," I conceded.

She laughed and said, "I'll also be able to look after you better there."

"Who says I need looking after?" I demanded.

"Oh, did I say that?" she asked. "I'm sorry. One only has to look at you to know that you can take care of yourself just fine."

I looked down at my torn and bloody shirt and decided to keep my mouth shut while I was behind.

"I hope I didn't bleed on your friend's upholstery," I told her.

"Don't worry. I'll clean it before I return the car."

She stopped the car in front of her building and said, "Now wait for me to come around and help you out."

"I can get out—" I started to protest.

She put her hand on my arm and said, "Humor me? I mean, who came out in the dead of night to pick you up?"

"Okay, I'll wait—but I carry the food," I said, holding onto the bag possessively.

"Deal."

I was glad that she was calling me "Jack" instead of "Miles." It meant that all of that forced formality was gone from between us.

We went up to her apartment, and she insisted that I sit on the couch while she got some cups and plates.

"I'll bring the food out here. I want you to relax."

"Okay, you're the boss."

She spread everything out on the coffee table and sat cross-legged on the floor opposite me. We laughed and giggled like two kids as we scooped food out of the cardboard cartons and drank beer out of paper cups.

"We should be eating this stuff with chopsticks, you know," she said at one point.

"I'd end up poking my eye out."

168

When we'd both eaten enough she put the rest of it on top of the stove in closed cartons and made some coffee. Over coffee she asked me to tell her what happened.

I gave her the whole story, leaving out the part about the gun. I don't know why; I just thought she didn't need to know about that.

She wasn't stupid, though.

"What about the gun?" she asked.

"What gun?"

"The one that's been digging into your back ever since you sat on the couch. The one we went back to the phone booth to find."

"How'd you know about that?" I asked.

"I know you. I know you don't like guns, but I also know that you wouldn't go up against this hit man without some kind of an edge."

"Yeah, big edge it turned out to be," I said, disgusted with myself. I pulled the holster from my belt and laid it down on the coffee table.

"Even with this he came out on top."

"At least he didn't kill you," she said, but then she had to add, "this time."

"Hey," I scolded her, "so he won round one. Do you know how many times I've lost the first round and still won the fight?"

"This is not a fight, Jack, this is your life!" she told me urgently. "I don't want to see you lose your life!"

"Don't worry, I won't."

"Sure, you also told me you were going to be careful, and look what happened," she said accusingly.

"I was careful."

"Well, it's a good thing you were lucky, too. Being careful like that can get you killed."

I hadn't realized it up until that point, but our voices had continued to rise until we were yelling at each other.

"Look, let's not fight," I told her.

"I want to fight," she snapped. "If I'm here fighting with you it means you're still alive, damnit, and that's the way I want you, Jack. Alive! Benny's not worth your getting killed!"

I think we were both shocked by her words, and we sat there and stared at each other. When the phone rang it startled us both.

She answered the phone by saying hello, listened for a moment, then held it out to me saying, "It's for you."

I took it from her, wondering who it was.

"Hello."

"I had nothing to do with that, Jacoby. You gotta believe me," a man's voice said.

It was him, the man from the fifth row.

"You were there?"

"I was late, but there wasn't nothing I could do," he insisted. "He must have followed you."

"He didn't follow me," I told him.

"You mean—"

"He must have spotted you and followed you there," I told him.

"Then if you hadn't come when you did, he might have killed me."

"I guess so. I hope you're not staying in the same place too long."

"Are you all right?" he asked, and I liked him better for remembering to ask.

"I got cut up some, but I'll live."

"You still want to help me?"

"I do."

"You could call it even now, you know," he told me. "I wouldn't blame you."

"You pick another time and place and I'll be there," I told him.

"I'll get back to you."

"Hey, what about telling me your name?"

"Later, I'll tell you later," he promised. "I'll call you."

"Wait—" I started, but he hung up.

"You're not going to meet him again," Julie said in an exasperated tone.

"Yes, I am," I answered.

She looked at me like I was crazy—or driving her crazy—and then picked up the empty coffee cups and carried them to the kitchen.

I sat back on the couch, staring at the phone, wondering about a few things.

How had he found out my name?

How had he known to call me at an office that was listed in the phone book under the name Eddie Waters?

And most of all, how had he known to call me at Julie's apartment, a number that wasn't even listed in the phone book?

CHAPTER FORTY

As much as I would have preferred to stay in bed all day—or, in this case, on Julie's couch—there were two people I had to see the next day. I had to talk to Hocus about Max the Ax's attempt to skewer me.

The other person I had to see was Benny. I couldn't put it off any longer, and Heck had already made the arrangements. And maybe it was time I faced my brother and asked him straight out if he killed Eddie. If he said no, maybe I'd believe him, and maybe I'd ask him if he saw anything or anybody while he was there.

I woke up to the smell of bacon and coffee and used the back of the couch to haul myself to a seated position. My throat ached and my side hurt, but it was a great feeling to wake up to another morning.

When she came walking into the living room carrying a cup of coffee, I had my feet on the floor and was contemplating getting up on them.

"What are you doing?" she demanded.

"I've got to get up," I told her.

"What for? You want to bust those stitches open?"

I shook my head, which did wonders for my neck.

"I've got to go see Benny, Julie. It's something I should have done days ago."

She set the coffee down on the table and said, "Well, at least have breakfast first. It's almost ready."

"Okay. Can you bring me some fresh clothes of Benny's?" I asked her.

"Sure."

When she brought me some of my brother's clothes I felt funny about having them on. Benny and I had shared clothing before, but we had never shared Julie before. I thought about that while I put on his clothes, and I still felt some guilt over it.

"Jack?"

"Yeah?" I said, becoming aware of the fact that she had been calling me for a few seconds.

"I said breakfast is ready."

"Okay, I'll be right there."

"Do you need any help?" she asked.

"No, I'm fine."

When she went back into the kitchen I struggled with a clean shirt, trying to get it on without stretching the stitches. The pants were easier because I put them on while I was sitting down. I slid my feet into my shoes and then walked into the kitchen.

"They fit?" she asked.

"We're about the same size," I pointed out.

She had set out some scrambled eggs, home fries, bacon, sausages and pancakes. I didn't have the heart to tell her I was still in training.

"I'm going to have to train extra hard for my next fight," I commented.

"Are you still going to fight, Jack?"

I started putting food in my plate and said, "I think so, Julie. I haven't really made up my mind yet, but I know I'll fight at least one more time."

"The Ricardi fight?"

"I'm surprised you know that."

"That's all Ben's been talking about for weeks," she told me. "How the Ricardi fight is a big stepping-stone for you."

"I guess he's right. Come to think of it, Ricardi just might make my mind up for me," I told her. "He's got a powerful right and could just knock me right out of the fight game."

"I don't think you ever really wanted to fight anyway, Jack. I think Ben forced you into it."

"I don't think 'forced' is exactly the right word," I told her, but I didn't elaborate.

It was funny, though, how she had made very much the

174

same observation that Willy Wells had made, that I didn't seem to have the desire it took to be successful in boxing—although neither one of them had said it in so many words.

Maybe the Ricardi fight would be my crossroads fight—if I managed to stay in one piece, and alive, until then.

When breakfast was over I said, "I have to get going."

"Where?"

"First I'm going to see Benny, then Detective Hocus. After that I'll start trying to find Max the Ax again."

She made a face.

"Such a ridiculous name for a dangerous man," she commented.

"I'll tell him your opinion when I see him," I promised.

As I got gingerly to my feet she said, "I'd make you promise to be careful, but you obviously aren't very good at keeping promises—especially that one."

"I promise," I said, raising my right hand, "I'll try not to get cut, slashed or killed."

"Just don't reach for your wallet too fast," she advised, "you'll rip those stitches."

"I'll keep that in mind. Oh," I said, remembering something, "if a man calls and he won't give his name, just take a message."

As I left she asked, "What if he says he's Max the Ax?"

"Take a number and tell him I'll get back to him as soon as hell freezes over."

CHAPTER FORTY-ONE

"I didn't kill him, Miles."

"Would you tell me if you did, Benny?" I asked him.

He looked at me and shrugged.

"I don't know," he answered, and I thought that at least that was honest. "I know how much he meant to you," he pointed out. "Probably more than I do, but I didn't kill him. I swear, Jack."

"Okay, Benny, okay."

"You and Julie have to believe me, and so does Delgado. I mean, if you don't believe me, who will?"

My brother was five years older than I was, but he looked about fifteen years older. In fact, he looked more like my father than my brother.

"You look like shit, Benny," I told him.

"Yeah," he said, running his fingers through his wild shock of hair, "I feel like shit, too. How's Julie?"

"She's fine."

"You taking care of her for me?" he asked, and there was such a trusting look on his face that suddenly I felt like shit, too.

"We're taking care of each other, Benny."

"Good. Why you moving so stiff, kid? You get hurt in the fight? And what happened to your neck? What the fuck you been doing to yourself?"

I told him some of the things I'd been doing to try and clear him, and I told him about being jumped on the street and about what had happened last night.

"Jesus Christ, kid, no wonder you ain't been in to see me," he said. "You been putting yourself through the wringer for me."

"Yeah, maybe," I said. I had gone through a lot trying to clear him, but all I could think about while I was sitting there was how I had slept with my brother's wife.

"Benny, I only came in to explain, so you wouldn't think I'd dumped you or something. I'm trying to get you out of here."

"I know, kid, I appreciate it. Listen, do you think that maybe next time you come in you could—you know, maybe just sneak in a drink or—"

"Shit, Benny, if nothing else good comes out of this maybe this will help you cut down on your drinking," I told him. "You know you were going at it pretty heavy before this happened."

"I know, I know," he said, wringing his hands, "but it seems like the closer we get to a title shot, the more my nerves need it, you know?"

"Benny, we're miles away from a title shot. Don't use that as an excuse to get drunk!" I snapped at him.

"All right, kid, don't come down on me now," he said.

"Jesus—" I started, but then I stopped myself. "Okay, I'm sorry. We'll talk about it when you get out."

"If I get out. You been trying, kid, I'll give you that, but you ain't come up with nothing that's going to get me out of here."

"I will, Benny. I'm not finished looking, and Heck's got another P.I. on the case, too."

Suddenly he laughed shortly and said, "It's funny."

"What's funny?"

"I never wanted you working as a P.I., and here you are doing it for me. That's funny."

"Yeah, I guess it is," I said, getting to my feet slowly.

"You're getting fat," he told me. "The Ricardi fight's coming up, you know. You better not be using this as an excuse to stuff yourself with junk food."

"I'll tell you what," I told him. "When you get out I'll make you a deal. No more booze for you, and no more junk food for me. What do you say?"

"You win the Ricardi fight, and I won't touch another drop," he said, making a counter offer.

"Okay, you're on."

"Uh, if I don't get out of here in time for the fight, you're going to need somebody in your corner," he said.

"That's all arranged."

"It is? Who'd you get?"

"Willy Wells."

"Jesus Christ, that old thief!" he snapped. "He didn't waste much time, did he?"

"He's the best there is, Benny, you said so yourself."

"I know, kid, I know. Ah, what the hell, you'll probably do better with him than you would with me, anyway."

"Benny, I've got to go. I have to talk to the police about last night."

"Yeah, okay. Look, take care of yourself, huh, kid?"

"Yeah, you too."

"Give Julie my love, will you? And don't let her come down here, okay? I don't want her to see me like this."

"I hear you."

I had started for the door when a thought occurred to me and I turned back.

"Benny?"

"Yeah, kid?"

"Benny, when you first started out, did you ever meet or hear about a trainer or manager named Corky Purcell?"

"Purcell?" he asked. "Purcell. It sounds familiar, but I can't think of it right now. Is it important?"

"It isn't for him anymore," I told him. "He's dead."

CHAPTER FORTY-TWO

"I told you to watch out!" Hocus shouted at me. "I warned you, and what do you do? You go out and get yourself sliced to fucking pieces! And then you don't even call the cops and report it!"

"I'm reporting it now," I reminded him.

"Damnit, Jacoby, that's not what I mean and you know it," he told me, getting all red in the face. "You should have called us as soon as it happened."

"As soon as it happened I was too busy bleeding, and panicking. I called the only number I could think of and went to a hospital. By that time it was so late I didn't figure it mattered whether I reported it last night or this morning."

"Well, it mattered!" he snapped. "Damnit, did you even get a look at his face?"

"No, it was too dark and it happened too fast."

"So you can't even swear that your assailant matched the description we got from Detroit on Max the Ax," he pointed out.

"Oh, shit, Hocus, are you going to tell me that you can't put a wanted alarm out on him based on this?" I asked, pointing to my throat. "He sure as hell had a sharp blade, I can testify to that firsthand."

"I can't assume it was him just because he had a sharp knife, and you know it!"

"Well, I—" I started to say, rising out of my chair, when my stitches pulled, halting me in mid-sentence.

I lowered myself back into my chair and started again in a softer, calmer tone of voice.

"You can't assume it was him, but I can," I told him.

"Which means you're still going to look for him," he said. "You're still going to try and get yourself killed."

"Yes to the first and an emphatic no to the second," I told him.

"You're not funny, Jacoby. In fact, I think you're dangerous—to yourself. Maybe I should slap you into protective custody."

"Oh, c'mon, Hocus, you know that went out with the hula hoop."

We both sat staring at each other, catching our breath. The other men in the room had been doing their best to ignore us, but we hadn't been making it easy for them.

"All right, look," he said, "I think you've pretty much established one thing."

"What?"

"Unofficially, I know as well as you do that it was Max the Ax who tried to carve you up, so I think you've pretty much established the fact that he's involved with your man in the fifth row."

I eyed him suspiciously.

"I'll agree with that, but that doesn't mean that he had nothing to do with Eddie Waters."

"You're reaching, Jacoby. You pulled this hit man in out of left field and connected him to one of your cases, but to connect him with both cases is just too much coincidence to ask for."

"Maybe," I said lamely, "and maybe not."

"Oh, that's a convincing argument," he said, sarcastically. "I can't argue with that."

"You're not so funny yourself, Hocus," I told him. I pushed myself to my feet very gently and said, "I'll be seeing you."

"Where are you going now?"

"I'm going to get you the proof you need," I told him.

"All right, wait a minute," he said, standing up and coming around the desk. "Look," he said in a lower voice, "if you're going to set up another meet with this guy from the fifth row, let me know, okay? I'll come in and back you up."

"I appreciate the offer, but if he spots you he won't trust me again."

"He won't spot me," he promised. "Besides, getting yourself cut up like that must have convinced him that you're on his side—but you could have thought of an easier way, you know?"

"Oh, I don't know. This seems to have a certain flair. I think it brought the point home pretty well, don't you?"

"Oh," he groaned. "Get the fuck out of here and take your puns with you."

"Okay, I'm going. I'll call you if I need you," I promised.

"Or if you get any information you think I can use," he added, "like where Max the Ax is staying. Don't try and take him alone, Jacoby. He's out of your league."

"So everyone keeps trying to tell me," I told him.

I left the precinct, wondering what the hell my next step should be. I could finally check out that hotel on Fourteenth Street where Louise claimed she saw Max, but I didn't think he'd be fool enough to go back there, if indeed that had been where he was staying.

I decided to go home and get into some of my own clothes. Being in Benny's still made me feel uneasy, like I was sleeping in his bed or something.

Seeing Benny hadn't eased my mind about any of this mess. I still felt guilty about having slept with Julie, and I felt even guiltier about not being sure if I believed Benny's story. Finding Max the Ax was my last chance to prove that Benny didn't kill Eddie. It was my last chance to believe him, because if none of Eddie's clients killed him, and Max didn't kill him, who did that leave?

CHAPTER FORTY-THREE

After changing into some fresh clothing of my own, I decided to go ahead and waste the time it would take to check out the hotel on Fourteenth Street; but first I stopped at my bank to pick up some funds, just in case I had to grease some palms. I also had to pay Tracy back the forty bucks she had loaned me.

It cost me twenty dollars of that money to get the desk clerk to let me look at the registration cards for the past week. Naturally, I didn't find anybody named Max "the Ax" Collins registered, and I hadn't expected to. What I was looking for was someone from Detroit, or at least someone with the same initials.

It's a proven fact, and one that no law enforcement agency can understand, that when choosing an alias criminals often use the same initials as in their real names. Very often they don't realize that they've done so. Eddie Waters had always pounded it into my head to look for those initials if I felt a man had any reasons for using a name other than his own.

I found a registration card for a man named Mark Costa who had registered the morning of my fight. His home was not listed as Detroit, but it was listed as a town I had never heard of in Michigan. Close enough.

The room number was 414, on the fourth floor.

"Is this man still registered?" I asked.

He took the card from me, scanned it briefly, then said, "Yeah, as far as I know."

"Do you know what that man looks like?" I asked.

The clerk was young, bearded, and not particularly well dressed, which wasn't surprising. The hotel was only one small notch above the Roger Williams, and the only real difference in this clerk's attitude, as opposed to the clerk in the Williams, was that this clerk probably couldn't have given a damn less what the Mets were doing.

He had been reading on OTB sheet when I interrupted him with my questions, and my twenty-dollar bill.

"Oh, man, do you know how many people I see in one day?" he asked me.

"Yeah, but this one wouldn't be a wino," I told him.

He looked around quickly and said, "Don't let the manager hear you say that, man. He don't allow no winos in here."

"You know what I mean, pal. Think back. Was this guy brown-haired, about five nine, kind of slim and college looking?"

"Shit, man, I may not have even been on the desk when he signed in, you know?"

"Yeah, okay. How much to get a look at his room?" I asked.

His eyes widened and he said, "A lot more than you could afford, brother. This may not be the best job in the world, but it's the only one I got."

"Fifty?" I said, letting him see the 50 on the bill in my hand.

He looked around quickly for the feared manager, and then said, "Fifty's just right." He grabbed for the bill, but I held tight.

"Passkey?"

He started looking left and right to such a degree that I thought he was shaking his head, but when he was satisfied that we were unobserved he slipped me the key and I handed him the fifty.

"Try and be quick about it, huh?" he asked.

"Quick as I can."

"If anything comes up, I'll ring the phone once."

"Okay."

I took the elevator to the fifth floor. The hallway was empty, so I took the gun out of the bloody holster that was clipped to my belt, held it in my right hand and unlocked the door with my left. I pushed the door open with a bang and jumped into the room with the gun held straight out in front of me.

Now, maybe I did it wrong. I mean, there could have been some innocent guy from Michigan in that hotel room with a broad, or maybe even saying his prayers. If there had been I would have been embarrassed and probably had a lot of explaining to do to the cops, but I would have been alive.

Then again, I could have just knocked on his door and caught a blade in the gut for my trouble.

This way, I was in control of the situation.

As it turned out, it didn't matter how I did it, because the room was empty.

I closed the door behind me and then holstered the gun. I gave the room a quick toss, but couldn't come up with anything that would tell me if the room had recently been inhabited by the hit man from Detroit.

What I did establish was that whoever had been living there had skipped without paying their hotel bill. There were no clothes and no personal effects to indicate that someone was presently living there.

Since the phone hadn't rung I decided to give the room a second time over, and that's when I turned up the small notebook under the phone. I didn't know whether it was left behind on purpose or not, but it told me what I wanted to know. Max the Ax had been staying here.

When I opened the small, blue-covered spiral notebook, what I saw on the first page froze me solid. There were three addresses written down. One was mine, one was the office address, and the other—well, the other one was the one that scared me and made me sure that this had been the Ax's room.

The third address was Julie's!

CHAPTER FORTY-FOUR

I grabbed up the phone and dialed Julie's number and became even more worried when there was no answer. It scared the shit out of me to think that the hit man knew where she lived. He could only know that from having followed me at one time or another, which was how he must have gotten all three addresses.

The only other way was if someone had given them to him.

I left the room, satisfied that he was gone and was not returning. I brought the key back to the clerk and told him to tell the manager not to depend on getting paid for Room 414.

I grabbed a passing cab when I left and had him take me home. When I got there I grabbed the phone and dialed Julie's number again.

This time she answered.

"Don't ask me any questions," I told her. "Just pack a bag and be ready to leave. I'm on my way over."

"Jack? What's the—"

"Julie, please, no questions. Just pack and be ready."

"You're scaring me," she complained.

"I'm trying to," I told her, and hung up.

When I hung up I dialed Missy's number and waited three rings until she answered.

"Hello, Missy, it's Jack."

"Hi, Jack. Listen, I'm sorry I didn't come to the office today—" she started, but I interrupted her.

"That's okay, Missy, don't worry about it. Listen, I need a favor."

"What is it?"

"Do you have a key to Eddie's apartment?"

She hesitated, then said, "Yes, I do. Why?"

"I want to use the apartment for a while," I told her. "I'm too easy a target here in my own place."

"A target? What are you talking about?"

I explained about being attacked and injured by Max the Ax, then told her that I was sure he knew where I lived.

"Are you going to hide out?" she asked.

"Not exactly, I just want somewhere to go where he won't find me. I don't think he'll look in Eddie's apartment for me."

I didn't tell her that I also had plans to leave Julie there too.

"All right, Jack, but you don't have to come out here to get my key. There's a key in Eddie's desk, right in the top drawer."

"Great!" I told her. "You're a doll, Missy, thanks."

"Jack, do you still want me to keep checking the client list?" she asked.

"Uh, no, I think we can forget that, Missy. In fact, you don't have to come to the office for a while if you don't want to."

"Will you be keeping it open?" she asked.

"I haven't decided yet, Missy, but I'll let you know soon."

I was in a hurry but didn't want to seem as if I were rushing her to hang up. Thankfully, though, she was the one who ended the conversation.

I packed a suitcase with some clothing, made sure I had my bankbook, and then went out to grab a cab and pick up Julie.

Julie was all packed and ready when I got there; and she carried her own bag down to the waiting cab, because she didn't want me straining my stitches.

"Now, what's this all about?" she asked in the backseat of the cab after I'd given the driver the office address.

"I'll tell you later, Julie. Just trust me for a little while," I told her. I didn't want to tell her anything until we were alone.

I had the cab wait in front of the office while I went up to get the key to Eddie's apartment. While I was there I also took the extra box of shells from the bottom drawer, along with the shoulder holster. I wasn't sure I'd be able to get the blood off the belt holster.

The cab ride ended in front of Eddie's building, which was

at Fifty-sixth Street and Second Avenue. I paid the cab driver and then refused to let Julie carry both bags. I did relent when it came to her bigger bag and let her carry that one.

"This isn't bad," she said when we were in Eddie's apartment. "A bit musty . . ." she started to say, but then stopped, realizing it was musty because it had been unused since Eddie's death.

"Why don't you make some coffee, and then I'll tell you why I brought you here."

"For immoral purposes, I hope," she said, and then went off to find the kitchen. I was very pleased with the offhanded way she had made that remark, and I felt very comfortable being there with her.

I took both bags into Eddie's bedroom and left them in the closet. On the floor of the closet I found a kit that he used to clean his guns and took it into the living room with me.

I set the kit up on the coffee table and started cleaning the gun and the belt holster. I set the shoulder holster on the couch next to me.

The smell of coffee was soon in the air, and it improved on the musty smell of the apartment. Julie came walking in carrying two cups of black coffee, put them on the coffee table, and then sat on the floor facing me, with the table between us.

"You getting your pistol ready for a shootout, Marshal?" she asked.

"That's right, Miss Kitty," I told her.

She rubbed her arms as if she had gotten a chill just then and said, "I'm making jokes because I'm scared, and seeing you clean that gun isn't helping any."

"I know," I told her. I put the rag and gun down and let my hands rest on my knees. I explained why I not only had to move myself, but her as well, and that scared her even more.

"Why would he have my address?" she asked.

"I guess it was just somewhere else to find me if he wanted me," I told her. "I'm sorry if I've put you in danger, Julie."

"Don't be silly, Jack. If you have it's only because you've been working to clear Benny."

"Yeah, Benny," I said, picking up the gun and rag again. She'd brought my brother into the room with us with that remark, and I started to feel uncomfortable with her again.

"Drink your coffee," she told me, and I looked at her and marveled at how beautiful she was to me. More than once I

191

had been on the verge of asking her why she had ever married Benny, and now I felt the urge again.

"So what are we going to do now, hide out here together?" she asked.

"Much as I'd like to, no. You're going to hide out here; I'm going to go and find the man again."

"Oh, Jack, haven't you had enough of him? Do you want to get killed?" she asked.

"Julie, this is my only chance to prove that Benny didn't kill Eddie. If I can catch this guy and get him to admit that he did it, Benny's free. Don't you want that?"

My last question was malicious. I wanted her to say no, she didn't want Benny free, she wanted him to stay in jail so she could be with me.

"Of course I want him free, Jack," she said instead. "How could you think otherwise."

"I don't," I assured her. "I don't think otherwise, that's why I'm going out there, to try and get you your husband back."

That seemed to put a damper on any further conversation, and she took the empty cups back to the kitchen to wash them.

I walked over to a highboy that stood against the wall that separated the kitchen from the living room and opened the top drawer, where I knew Eddie had kept another gun. This one was a German gun, a Heckler & Koch P9 that Eddie was very fond of. It was lighter than the .38, but held nine shots to the .38's six. It was a 9mm with its own holster, a shoulder rig. I decided right then and there that this was the gun I'd carry from now on, figuring the more shots I had, the better. I took it back to the coffee table with me and proceded to clean it.

"Another one?" Julie asked, walking back into the room.

"Yep. This one's mine, the other one is yours," I told her, indicating the automatic I was cleaning.

"Mine? I don't want a gun. I don't know how to use one," she protested.

"You will before I leave here. It's very simple," I assured her. "Come here."

She came over to me and I stood up behind her, placing the .38 in her hand, and putting down the automatic.

"Hold the gun with both hands," I told her, putting my hands over hers. "If anybody comes through that door and it isn't me, just point the gun and start pulling the trigger. Keep pulling it until it's empty. It's as simple as that."

"Simple?" she asked. "To kill a man?"

"If he's trying to kill you, yes."

"Have you ever killed anyone?"

"You know I haven't, but if I had been able to get off a decent shot last night, I might have."

I put the .38 down on the table and began cleaning the 9mm again.

"Is there food in the kitchen?" I asked.

"Are you hungry?"

"I just want to make sure you don't have to go out for anything. Check the refrigerator and the closets, let me know if you need anything."

She went off to take inventory, and I stood up and took off my jacket so I could try on the shoulder holster. I had some trouble getting it on because I was being careful of my stitches, but I finally got it into place and then tried the gun in the holster. The fit was good and I slid my jacket back on over it just as Julie came back into the room.

"There's plenty of food," she assured me.

"Good. Don't leave this apartment for any reason, Julie," I told her.

"I feel like I'm in—" she started to say, but stopped before she could say the word *jail*. I guess she thought it would have been in bad taste, considering Benny's position.

"I'll call you periodically to make sure everything is all right," I told her.

"Good, at least that way I'll know that you're all right."

"I'll let the phone ring twice, then hang up, then call back. Don't answer it otherwise."

"Okay, I'll—oh, God, the phone," she said suddenly.

"What about it?"

"At my place, you got a phone call. It was from that man you've been looking for."

"Why didn't you tell me before?" I asked.

"I haven't had a chance to. You've been rushing me so much that I just didn't think—"

"Okay, forget that. What did he say?"

"He said he wanted to meet you again and that he'd call you at your office at eight o'clock tonight."

I looked at my watch and saw that it was only five, so I had three hours to hit the streets and then get back to my office.

My office? That thought had come pretty easily.

"That gives me three hours," I said aloud.

"To do what?"

193

"To do whatever has to be done," I told her. "Just sit tight and don't worry. Everything is going to be fine."

"Yeah, just swell." She looked over at Eddie's TV and said, "Well, at least he's got cable." I don't think she realized that she was talking as if Eddie were just away on a vacation.

"Lock this door behind me," I told her, "and remember, don't answer the phone unless I ring twice first, and don't answer the door. I won't knock, because I'll have the key. If somebody knocks, that means its not me and you pick up that gun. Do you understand?"

"You're scaring me again," she said.

"Julie—" I began, wanting to take her in my arms, but I stopped myself and said, "just lock the door after I leave, okay?"

"Okay. Be careful."

"I will."

When I got to the street I was kind of at a loss as to where to go next. Where do you find a hit man in New York City when he doesn't want to be found? He could be anywhere.

He could be right behind me, following me.

That thought gave me a chill, and I looked up and down the street. There were plenty of pedestrians, but none fit the description I'd gotten from Hocus.

I began to walk downtown on Second Avenue, wondering who might have given Collins those three addresses if he hadn't gotten them by following me. Obviously, the night that he'd tried to carve me up, he had been following the man from the fifth row, not me. And speaking of the man from the fifth row, how had he gotten all of those phone numbers? My home, the office, and Julie's?

I started to think about that more and more. The man was an old trainer, old in both senses of the word. He had to be over sixty years of age, and he had to have been working in the fight game years ago. Corky Purcell must have been a contemporary of his and had been trying to help him, obviously. He also ended up getting killed for it. What if there were other contemporaries of his trying to help him? If there were, who would they be? Somebody about the same age, who had also been working in the fight game a long time and who also knew me well enough to have those three phone numbers.

As one specific name came to mind, I felt that I had finally gotten a break in the case of the man in the fifth row.

CHAPTER FORTY-FIVE

Willy Wells, that was the name I came up with, and I pretty much knew where to find him. Willy hardly ever left the gym on Forty-second Street until after six o'clock.

Willy was well over sixty, although he was a feisty old guy who would probably bury a good number of the young fighters he was training and go on to find even younger ones. He was a Ray Arcel type who would probably still be training fighters when he was ninety.

If Corky Purcell or his friend, the now infamous "Man in the Fifth Row," were trainers of any renown at all, Willy had to have known them when they were in the business, and probably knew them now.

Willy knew my home number, he knew my office number, and he knew Julie's number, because that day I had worked out with his fighter and agreed to let him work my corner in the Ricardi fight, the last thing I had done before leaving the gym was give him those three phone numbers.

He in turn had to have passed them on to the mystery man from row five.

Now all I had to do was get Willy to talk, to tell me the man's name and where I could find him before the killer found him again.

When I got to the gym it was uncommonly quiet. Willy usually had one or two of his fighters stay and work out overtime. For the place to be this quiet at five-thirty was uncommon . . . and suspicious.

When I walked in and found it so quiet I quelled my first instinct, which was to call out Willy's name. Instead, I pulled the little 9mm from the holster and started working my way toward the main light switch. If the killer was there I had the edge because I knew the layout and he didn't. Once I had doused all of the lights my edge would grow a little bigger, and I needed as much of one as I could get.

Before reaching the main switch I passed a pay phone and decided to call Hocus and get him the hell over here; only when I picked up the receiver I found that the cord had been cut cleanly, as if with something very sharp. I knew then that there were two possibilities: the killer had either been there and gone, or he was still there.

Walking as softly as I could, and listening intently, I made my way to the master switch, and just as I reached it I heard a sound that plucked at my nerves as if they were guitar strings.

I heard a man's moan as it stretched out and rose to a high whine, and then a scream.

I knew it was Willy Wells screaming, and that's when I hit the switch, plunging the whole works into darkness.

Willy's scream was cut short suddenly, and I knew that the killer realized that somebody else was in the gym with them.

I decided that my best play was not to move. The killer knew of only one way out, and that was the way he had come in, which would have been the front door. There was one other exit, a fire exit, but you couldn't find it with the lights on unless you knew where it was, and in the dark it was impossible, especially if you were unfamiliar with the layout.

My best play was just to sit and wait for him to try and make the door.

I crouched down, which didn't help my stitches any, but I wanted to make myself as small a target as I could. I had the feeling that although Max was a blade man, his last encounter with me might have prompted him to start carrying a gun, just in case we met again.

Gradually my eyes began to get used to the darkness, and I assumed he would also wait for his to adjust. He was, after all, a pro, and he wasn't about to make any rash moves.

Willy's screams had to have come from the locker room, and there was only one exit from the locker room to the main gym area. He was going to have to come from that doorway.

I had a general idea of where that doorway was, but it was too dark for me to make it out. The front door, on the other hand, had a certain amount of light filtering in from outside and was easy to spot in the darkness. I had made up my mind to fire at any shadow or silhouette that passed in front of the door and ask questions later.

After ten minutes—or maybe it was twenty or thirty—I began to realize that we were both playing the same waiting game. He was waiting for me to come in, and I was waiting for him to come out. I thought I had the edge because I was out, but he had the edge because he'd probably been through this before. What I'm trying to say is that after waiting all that time my nerves were starting to go, which was probably what he was counting on.

Suddenly I realized what a prize dope I had been. Since the man was a pro one of the first things he had probably done was locate the main light switch. He knew I had turned out the lights, and I was crouched right under the master switch, which meant that he probably knew exactly where I was!

I started to sweat freely and made a monumental effort not to panic. I had to move away from there to a spot he'd never expect me to be. I had to move away from the wall entirely, and I thought I knew of a good spot.

Ring center.

I started to crawl on all fours toward the ring, trying not to scrape the gun or my feet on the floor. When I reached the ring apron I paused to listen, but if he was moving he was doing so with the ease of a cat, because I couldn't hear anything but my own breathing, which sounded tremendously loud in my ears.

I tried not to grunt from the pain as I hoisted myself up onto the ring apron, causing my stitches to pull. Once on the apron I crawled under the ropes and out to the center of the ring, where I stayed on my belly.

I had made it to where I wanted to be, and now I suddenly felt like a perfect target. What if he had second-guessed me? What if I had done exactly what he wanted me to do?

What if he was gone?

What if I had been making a complete asshole of myself, waiting in the dark for a man who was already gone, crawling around on my hands and knees for no reason.

Sure, the fire exit was hard to find, but the killer was in the locker room with Willy, wasn't he? All he had to do was ask

197

Willy if there was another way out. I was sure that Willy would have been only too happy to show the man the way out.

So what do you do now, stupid? I asked myself. Lie here on your belly the whole night, or make a move?

And what if I was wrong? What if he was just waiting for me to make a move so he could shove a shiv into me, or pump a few slugs into me?

I'd never know until I made up my mind.

Very slowly I made my way back to the master switch. Maybe the last thing he would expect me to do would be to put the lights back on. Maybe I'd catch him in the middle of the floor, like a cockroach crawling across the kitchen floor in the middle of the night when he thinks everyone is asleep.

What if . . .

I put my sweaty hand on the switch, holding the gun out in front of me with my other hand, and pulled.

The place was bathed in light, and I had a moment of sheer panic as I realized that I was totally blinded by the light. I dropped my hand from the switch and attempted to shade my eyes and regain some degree of sight, all the while waiting for the impact of a knife or a bullet to drive the life out of me.

Nothing like that happened, and, as my sight gradually returned, I could see that no one was there.

I was alone.

And feeling stupid.

I got up and walked around the ring to the entrance to the locker room. Very slowly, with the gun held ready, I eased through the door until I could see inside.

Willy Wells was lying on the floor, his knees drawn up to his chest like a fetus. I controlled the urge to rush to him and made a complete survey of the room. When I was satisfied that no one but Willy and myself were in there, I went to him, hoping that all of my care and time-consuming caution had not caused him to die.

"Willy?" I called, rolling him over.

The tough little man's wrinkled face was pale and clouded with pain.

"Shit, man, I hurt, I hurt all over," he said from between clenched teeth.

"Stay still, Willy, I'll get an ambulance."

"I didn't tell him nothing, Jack. I swear, I didn't tell him nothing," he told me urgently.

"I know you didn't, Willy. Keep quiet now."

"Nothing, I told him nothing," he said again, and one hand reached out like a small claw and grabbed ahold of my sleeve. "But you gotta know," he told me, "you gotta know what he knows, Jack."

"What's that, Willy? What do I have to know?"

"The name, the name..." he said, his voice fading out so that I couldn't hear him.

"What name, Willy?" I asked, leaning closer. "What's the name?"

"——layne," I heard him say, catching only the last half of the name."

"Again, Willy, again," I urged him.

"——layne," I heard again and then, just before he passed out on me, he mustered up what strength he had left and said out loud, "Trelayne!"

Trelayne! I had a name now, something to go on.

He was out cold, but he was still alive. If he was going to stay that way I had to get him an ambulance. I walked over to the pay phone that was by the fire exit, hoping that the killer hadn't also cut the cord on that one. I was in luck; the cord was still attached. Apparently he hadn't been able to find the phone any more than he'd been able to find the fire exit. The metal bar that locked the door on the inside was still in place, and—

Jesus! The implication of that hit me like a wet towel. The fire door was locked on the inside!

I turned around so fast I felt the stitches in my side go. As I felt the blood seeping out and soaking into my shirt, I saw that one of the lockers was now open where all of them had been closed when I entered.

He had been in one of the lockers, and now he was gone!

CHAPTER FORTY-SIX

"Well, at least this one's still alive," Hocus told me as we watched the ambulance attendants carry Willy Wells out on the stretcher. We were outside the locker room, where there was a lot of activity, and another attendant was putting a fresh bandage on my side. I hadn't ripped the stitches, but I'd stretched them enough to need a new dressing.

"Yeah, maybe just barely," I pointed out.

He looked at me and said, "You can't take the blame for that, son."

"Yeah, well, maybe if I hadn't been playing hide and seek in the dark and had gotten to a phone sooner—"

"That's second-guessing yourself. Personally, I think you played it wrong, but it's done and you can't go back and do it again," he told me.

I glanced at him and said, "What did I do wrong?"

"You really want to know?"

"I asked, didn't I?" I said as the attendant finished me up. I put my shirt back on and buttoned it. "Thanks," I told the guy.

Hocus and I went over and leaned on the ring apron, and he lit up a cigar before speaking.

"Okay, aside from the fact that you should have turned right around, left and called me the minute you smelled trouble, shutting the house lights was dumb."

"Why?"

"Think about it, Jacoby," he told me, prodding me on the head with a thick forefinger. "The man had no idea you were here. You shut the lights and tipped him right off."

"Uh-huh," I said, refusing to admit that he was right and I was wrong. "*I* knew that *he* was here, and since I knew the layout, shutting the lights should have given me an edge on him. Besides, the lights could have gone out for any number of reasons."

"Okay, so you're not so dumb, but assuming that the man was armed with a gun was an error in judgment. He's a blade man and he wouldn't be caught dead with a gun!" he explained.

"So that's why I didn't get shot in the back while he was inside the locker."

"Right. Apparently, rather than try to sneak up on you while you were on the phone and slit your gizzard, he decided to run and fight another day."

"Which was probably lucky for one of us," I said.

"Uh, yeah, for one of you," he said, leaving no doubt that he thought I was the lucky one. He got up and walked away, back to the locker room, and I followed, tucking in my shirt.

"What have we got?" he asked his partner.

"I think our man made a mistake," Wright replied. He had something in his hand, and he handed it to Hocus.

"What is it?" I asked over his shoulder.

He gave me a long, slow look and said, "Well, let me look at it and then I'll show it to you."

"Let's look at it together," I proposed.

He threw me a look of pure exasperation and then turned around and opened his hand so we could both see what was in it.

It was a Howard Johnson's matchbook.

"That must be where he's staying now!" I said, grabbing it out of his hand in my excitement.

"Don't jump to conclusions," Hocus told me. He turned to Wright and asked, "Where'd you find it?"

"In the locker Jacoby says he was hiding in," Wright told him. "Our man must have dropped it by accident."

"Right!" I said enthusiastically.

"Yeah, he dropped it, all right," Hocus said, "but whether or not it was an accident remains to be seen."

"What do you mean?" I asked.

"This may have been meant for you to find," he said, taking

the book of matches back and shaking it under my nose, "and not us."

"You mean, he wants me to go there looking for him?"

"Maybe," he said again, "but what he wants and what he gets are going to be two very different things." He turned back to his partner and asked, "Where's the nearest Howard Johnson's motel?"

"Eighth Avenue," I answered first, "and Fifty-third."

Hocus looked at me as if he was surprised I was still there and said, "Well, we'll check it out."

"We'll all check it out," I told him.

"Jacoby—"

"Either I go with you, or I'll try and get there ahead of you, Hocus," I told him.

"Jesus . . ." he said, and looked at his partner, who shrugged helplessly.

"All right, let's go," he said. As I started to walk out of the locker room he backhanded me on the shoulder to get my attention.

"Hey!"

"What?"

"You got a permit for that gun?" he asked, indicating the 9mm under my arm. He couldn't see it, but it had been a part of my story that I'd told him when he arrived.

I hesitated a moment, then said, "Uh, well, no, not really."

"Well, Jesus Christ, just don't shoot anybody, huh?" he said. Then as he was brushing by me he added, "If you don't have to."

CHAPTER FORTY-SEVEN

We drove to the Howard Johnson's in Hocus and Wright's unmarked car, with Wright driving.

"Jesus Christ," I told Hocus, who was in the front seat next to Wright, "he drives like an old lady. Hey, Wright, why don't you use the siren?"

He moved his shoulders like he was shivering at the thought and told me, "It's too embarrassing. All those people looking at you," he said, and then snorted.

"You're uptight, Jacoby," Hocus told me. "Using the siren would let the Ax know that somebody other than you got his message. Just relax and do me a favor."

"What?"

"Don't touch that gun, okay?"

We walked into the Howard Johnson's with me trailing behind the two detectives. They were official, and I was just along for the ride.

Hocus flashed his shield and told the clerk to produce the registration cards for the past few days. We went through them and all decided on one signed "Matt Cannon."

"Second floor," Hocus said, and handed the cards back.

"Stay away from that phone," Wright told the clerk as we started for the elevator.

"Why didn't you ask the clerk if he was in?" I asked.

"It don't matter," Wright said. "If he isn't, we'll just wait for him, and if he is, we'll know soon enough."

It sounded like pisspoor police procedure to me, but they were the pros.

I stood back as they drew their guns and positioned themselves, one on each side of the door.

"Hit it," Hocus told Wright.

"Aren't you supposed to identify yourselves or something?" I asked.

Wright threw me a pitying look just seconds before he hit the door with his foot. It flew open and they leaped into the room and out of sight. I didn't hear any shooting, so I went in after them.

They were both standing in the middle of the room, Hocus scratching his head and Wright standing with his hands on his hips.

"Cleared out," Wright said.

I looked around and saw what they meant. All the chest drawers were open and empty, and the same was true for the closet.

"He must have seen us coming," Wright said.

"Or he might have hung around outside the gym to see if we'd show up there," Hocus suggested. "Then he hotfooted it over here and cleared out."

"That's two hotel bills he's skipped on," I told them. They both looked at me and I asked, "Doesn't he know that's against the law? The man could get himself in serious trouble."

Hocus pointedly ignored me and asked Wright, "What now?"

"Trelayne," I said.

They both looked at me and Hocus said, "What?"

"Trelayne," I repeated. "The name Willy Wells gave me before he passed out on me."

"You said you didn't know the name," Hocus pointed out.

"No, but I know somebody who might."

"Who?"

I took them to Packy's and explained that Packy was an old pug, and as such he might remember the name and maybe better than that, the man.

When we got to Packy's he was behind the bar. I took Hocus and Wright to the bar and said, "Packy, meet a couple of friends of mine. Detectives Hocus and Wright." As he shook hands with each of them in turn I said, "That one's Hocus, and that one's Wright."

"Three beers?" Packy asked.

"Fine," Hocus said.

"Do you have a grapefruit juice?" Wright asked.

Packy gave him a funny look, but produced a cold glass of grapefruit juice.

Wright held it aloft and told us "It isn't just for breakfast anymore" before draining it.

"Packy, I've got a name to bounce off of you. I want to see if it rings any bells with you."

He leaned his powerful forearms on the bar and said, "Go ahead, hit me with your best shot."

"Trelayne."

Packy's eyes took on a look I'd never seen there before, and he straightened right up.

"Right between the eyes," Hocus said out of the side of his mouth.

"C'mon, Packy, who is he?" I asked.

"I ain't heard that name in years," Packy told us.

"How many?" Hocus asked.

"The story goes back almost twenty," he said.

"And how does the story go?" Hocus asked.

Packy started cleaning the already spotless bar with a rag while he spoke.

"It was in Chicago. Trelayne was managing an up-and-coming heavyweight, and he was approached to have his boy go in the tank."

"Throw a fight," I explained to the two detectives.

"I know what it means," Hocus told me, sounding annoyed. "Go ahead," he told Packy.

"The guy who approached Trelayne was the other kid's father—and he was connected."

"A wise guy?" Hocus asked.

"Mafia," I told Packy.

"I know what that means," Packy told me. "Yeah, the Mafia," he told Hocus.

"So Trelayne crossed him and the wise guys have been after him for twenty years for that?" Hocus asked. "I don't buy that."

"That ain't all of it. Trelayne didn't tell his boy about the offer, and his boy went out and fought his heart out. He knocked that boy out in the fourth round, and I mean he knocked him cold—and that kid just never woke up."

"He killed him," I said. Hocus threw me another annoyed look, and Packy just said, "Yup."

"So it's not really the Mafia that's been chasing this guy for twenty years," Hocus said, "it's the dead kid's father, who just happens to be a wise guy."

"He ain't really in the Mafia," Packy clarified, "but he's connected."

"What's the father's name?" I asked.

Packy shrugged.

"Trelayne would be the one who knows that," he answered. "Why are you asking questions about Trelayne? Jeez, I didn't even know he was still alive. He'd be an old geezer right about now."

"About as old as Willy Wells," I said.

"Right."

"And Corky Purcell."

"Purcell?" Packy said. "Is he around, too?"

"Not anymore, Packy," I said, paying him for the drinks, "not anymore."

CHAPTER FORTY-EIGHT

It was almost eight and my office looked as foggy as Sherlock Holmes's London, only this fog was man-made. Hocus's cigars and Wright's cigarettes were making it positively unlivable in there, and I was wishing to shit the damned phone would ring.

When we left Packy's we finally knew whom we were looking for, and why Max the Ax was looking for him, too. He'd been hired by this long-dead fighter's father to find Trelayne and kill him.

How had the father known that Trelayne was in New York?

That was something we might find out later. Right now our problem was finding Trelayne before the hit man did, and Hocus had figured out how to do that.

"We've got to make a target out of him," he said on the way to my office.

"How?" I asked. "The man's scared shitless."

"You've got to talk him into it, Jacoby," he told me. "If he calls here tonight it's because he trusts you. He'll listen to you if you tell him that it's the only way."

"The man's been running for twenty years," I told him. "What makes you think he's going to stop and paint a target on his back now?"

"Twenty years is an awful long time to run," Hocus pointed out. "This guy ain't got many years left if he's as old as you say. Maybe he'd like to spend his last few years in one spot, without looking over his shoulder."

"I guess," I agreed.

"Hey, don't you have a bottle of something in a file drawer?" Hocus asked.

I gaped at him and said, "Are you for real?"

That's when the phone rang.

"Private investigator," I said, still not sure how to answer the phone.

"Is it you?" he asked.

"Yes, it's me," I told him. Hocus had suggested that I don't let on right away that I knew his name. It might scare him off.

"Have you picked out a place to meet yet?" I asked.

"Uh-uh, I've decided not to meet you. I think I'm better off on my own."

"Wrong," I told him, "you're dead wrong, friend. You need all the help you can get."

"No," he said again, "I'm better off by myself. I appreciate your offer, but no thanks."

I was losing him. He was about to hang up unless I could do something or say something to prevent it.

"Trelayne, don't hang up!" I shouted. Hocus looked up at the ceiling, and when he looked back at me I held up my hand to him, indicating that it was all right.

"What did you call me?"

"I called you by your name, Trelayne. I know who you are."

"How—could you know that?" he stammered.

"Willy Wells told me."

"Willy!" he snapped. "I trusted him."

"And you were right to," I told him. "Right now Willy is in the hospital because he wouldn't tell a hit man where you were."

I didn't know that for sure, but what else could I tell him? Willy had told me that he hadn't told the Ax anything, but I couldn't be sure he hadn't cracked under the ministrations of the man's blade.

"Willy's in the hospital? What happened to him?"

"He was tortured by the man who's after you, but he didn't tell him anything."

"How'd he tell you my name, then?" he asked suspiciously.

"I found him and he figured my knowing your name would give me a head start on the hit man. He knew that if I found you first, you'd stay alive."

He was silent for a few moments, then he said, "First Corky, now Willy. I'm getting all my friends killed, ain't I?"

"Willy's not dead, Trelayne, but we don't know just how bad he's hurt yet."

"Creep," he said, but I knew he didn't mean me.

"What do you want me to do?" he asked.

"I want you to meet me," I told him.

"Where?"

"Somewhere where there's a lot of people and we can talk without fear of being knifed to death—not in a crowd, anyway."

"So where?"

"Grand Central Station," I told him. "By the information desk. I've got a proposition for you, a way that you can stop running. If you're interested."

"I'm interested," he told me. "I'm tired of running."

"Okay, let's make it nine o'clock tomorrow morning," I told him. "The place will be mobbed at that time."

"How will I know you?" he asked.

"I've got a bandage around my neck to go with the one over my eye," I told him. "Compliments of your friend and mine."

"All right," he said, "I'll be there."

"Don't come until nine," I told him. "I'll get there first."

"O-Okay, Mister. I'm trusting you with my life."

"Don't worry," I told him, "you're in good hands." I sounded more confident than I felt.

When I hung up Hocus looked at me and said, "Grand Central? The Ax could sidle up right next to you and slip a shiv between your ribs before you knew it. You wouldn't even fall until the rush-hour crowd thinned out."

"Well, you won't let that happen," I told him. I repeated what Trelayne had just said to me. "I'm putting my life in your hands."

I was hoping he'd say something that would fill me with confidence.

He said, "Shit."

CHAPTER FORTY-NINE

Grand Central Station is one of my least favorite places in the world—not that I've been too many places in the world, but I can think of a whole lot of other places I'd rather be, especially at 9 A.M. or 5 P.M.

Boxing is one of the few one-on-one sports, and I'm much more comfortable in the ring with one other guy—not counting the ref—than I was standing in the middle of Grand Central Station with a sea of people around me—especially when one of them might be out to kill me.

I got to the information booth at about eight-fifty and just stood there looking battered and bandaged, ogling the endless stream of secretaries with short skirts and tight tops.

After the first few minutes I gave up trying to pick Trelayne out of the crowd and started trying to find Hocus and Wright. I didn't have any luck there either, but I hoped to hell they were out there somewhere with their eagle eyes on me.

At nine-ten I started to get worried, but as the big Longines clock struck nine-eleven a tall, gray-haired drink of water in a suit that looked ten years old approached me tentatively; and he was either my man, or he was going to ask me for a handout.

"Are you Jacoby?" he asked, looking furtively at the large crowds of people surrounding us.

"Yeah. Trelayne?"

He took a good look at me, taking in the acres of bandages I was wrapped in, and said, "You're all fucked up, aren't you?"

213

"That's a nice thing to say to a man who's trying to help you stay alive," I commented.

He smiled, showing me yellow teeth, and said, "Just like I did for you the other night."

I touched the bandage over my eye and said, "Right. C'mon, let's walk."

"Where?" he asked nervously.

"Just around," I said. "We'll walk in a circle. C'mon, he's not going to try for either one of us with all of these people around."

"Do you think he's here?"

I shrugged.

"He was on one of us that night under the highway. He may have been on one of us now and followed us here. That's why I wanted all these people around."

I moved away from the information booth and started walking toward Lexington Avenue. He hesitated a moment, then hurriedly caught up with me.

"What's this plan you got?" he asked me. Then before I could answer he said, "You got a cigarette?"

"I don't smoke."

"I ran low on funds," he told me.

I walked him over to a magazine stand and bought him a pack of Camels. When he had one lit up we continued walking.

"Okay," he asked again, "so what's this plan?"

"In effect, I want to paint a target on your back and then grab the hit man when he tries to hit it," I told him.

"That's cute," he said, assuming that I was joking.

"I wanted to be honest with you."

"You mean, you're not kidding? This is on the level?" he asked. "What do you think, I'm crazy?"

"I think you're tired of running," I told him, "and I'm offering you a way that you can stop."

He frowned and then asked, "Is there more to this great plan?"

"Not much," I answered. "It'll be me and the cops covering you in a location that we'll pick. We'll have to assume that the hit man is following either you or me, so we'll go to the location virtually at the same time, so that he's not there alone with either one of us."

"Then after he kills me you'll grab him," he finished.

"No, before he can even touch you we'll grab him. There are a couple of other murders the cops want to talk to him

214

about, and maybe they can get the name of the guy he's working for."

"I know who he's working for," he pointed out.

"Well, we're ninety-nine percent sure he's working for the man who approached you twenty years ago to have your fighter throw a bout."

"Willy told you about that, huh?"

"No, we got the story from someone else who was around the fight game back then. How the hell have you stayed out of sight for all these years, and why surface now?"

He shrugged.

"I'm tired of running, you know that. I wanted to come out in the open again, even if it was only for one night, so I got Corky to let me use his ticket and went to the Garden that night. The rest is history. Somebody must have spotted me, and the next thing I know some guy with a knife is on my tail."

"And then I started asking questions, trying to find out who sent me that advice. Whoever is after you wanted to get me out of the way before I could find you. What's the guy's name, Trelayne?"

"Oh, no," he told me. "The guy's mad enough at me as it is, if I gave you his name and you gave it to the cops—uh-uh, no way. You catch this hit man, and then if he doesn't give you the name, maybe I will; but even then I'll need some guarantees."

"It would be a lot easier if you would give us his name now," I pointed out to him.

"Sorry," he said shortly, and that was that.

We had circled around and were now walking toward the Vanderbilt Avenue side of the station.

"Where are we gonna do this?" he asked. "And when?"

"I've given that a lot of thought, and I think I have a good place. The cops can get us the okay."

"Where?"

"The Felt Forum," I told him, which was the part of Madison Square Garden where they had held the fight that night. Hocus could get official okays from the police and Garden officials.

"The cops can be all over the place and still be out of sight."

"Do you think this guy is gonna fall for this?" he asked.

"I hope so. We arranged to meet once and he was there, so I'm counting on its happening again."

"You're hoping," he repeated. "I think I'm crazy to go along

215

with this, but you got one thing right. It would be a relief to get this over with."

"Okay, so it's settled. We'll make the arrangements, and hopefully we'll be able to go tonight."

"Tonight?"

"The sooner the better, Trelayne," I told him.

"I guess."

"Call me at my office later today, at six. I'll let you know if it's on for tonight, and if not I'll let you know when. Okay?"

"I still say I'm crazy, but okay."

As we reached the wide staircase that led to the Vanderbilt Avenue exit I asked him, "Listen, how did you first learn that I was looking for you?"

"I, uh, Willy Wells told me when I first called him. He also said I could trust you; that's why I called you the first time."

"I see," I said. Pointing up the stairs, I told him, "Go out this way, hop in a cab and tell the driver you're being followed. He's a hack driver—he'll know what to do."

"I thought we wanted this guy to follow me?" he asked.

"Not right now," I told him. "I'd rather have him follow me now, which is what I'm going to try to do. When I leave here I'm going to walk downtown, making it very easy for him to tail me."

"What if he just goes ahead and kills you?" he asked, more with curiosity than concern.

"I'm betting he won't. He had his chance last night at the gym, and he passed it up," I explained. "The only time he really tried for me was under the highway, when he had you and me in the same place at the same time. I think he'll wait for that situation to arise again."

"You hope."

"Trelayne, I'm betting both our lives on it."

"Don't remind me. Uh, listen—"

"Yeah?"

"What if this guy spots the cops and takes off? He's gonna know we set him up, he's gonna be pissed. If he's gonna kill me I'd rather he did it quick. If he's mad, he might make it last—"

"All right, calm down. I've got another idea, but I didn't think you'd go for it."

"What is it?"

"Well, I'll set up the meet with the cops for nine-thirty, but you and I will get there at nine o'clock. When Collins gets

216

there, whether he's following me or you, he won't see any cops, because they won't come until later."

"Jeez—" he said, and I thought he'd balk, but he surprised me. "Okay, Kid. If I'm gonna trust you I'll trust you all the way. At least the cops'll show up in time to grab him."

"And if something does go wrong, in time to keep him from killing us."

"You hope," he said.

Again I told him, "We're betting our lives on it, pal."

CHAPTER FIFTY

I went to Eddie's apartment to have lunch with Julie and to await a phone call from Hocus telling me that all of the arrangements had been made.

Hopefully.

I was hoping to put this whole thing to bed tonight.

Talk about bed, Julie brought about definite thoughts in that direction as she looked particularly fetching in a hooded, maroon terry-cloth robe. She had explained that since she wasn't going out, she had decided there was no reason to get dressed. I had no complaints about that. I enjoyed the way her large breasts moved beneath the robe and the way her large nipples made their presence very obvious.

Leaving Grand Central Station, I still had not been able to spot either Hocus or his partner, but I was sure—almost—that they were there. I had drifted up the steps after Trelayne and watched him get into a cab, and had not seen anyone who looked like they might be following him. After that I walked uptown instead of downtown and stopped at a pay phone to call Julie and tell her I was bringing lunch. At no time while walking or while I was on the phone was I able to spot anyone following me. If the guy was tailing me, he was damned good at it.

I stopped in at a Charles & Co. and bought some cold cuts and bread for lunch.

"Ah," she said when I walked in, "a gourmet lunch."

I was pleased to see that she had the gun in her hand when I walked in. She had picked it up when she heard what sounded like the key in the lock.

"Just to be on the safe side," she explained, putting the gun down when she saw it was me.

"Good girl."

I was glad that I had scared her sufficiently enough to make her careful.

"How did it go?" she asked, emptying out the Charles & Co. bag on the table and laying out the spread.

"Okay, I guess. Trelayne showed up. I don't know for sure about Max or about Hocus. I couldn't spot either one."

I'd explained it all to her the night before, just before she went to sleep in the bedroom and I went to sleep on the couch. This was done by unspoken agreement, and speaking for myself it wasn't all that easy to forget that she was just a room away.

"Suppose that happens in the Forum?" she asked. "Suppose you think Hocus and his partner are there, but they're not?"

"Please," I told her, giving her a pained look, "don't even think it."

"Well, I wish you would think about it and reconsider," she told me.

"Julie, we went through this last night; let's not go through it again."

She didn't speak after that, but she started banging things around as she prepared lunch, then banged a sandwich down in front of me.

"Geez," I said, half aloud, "it feels like we're married."

She whirled around on me and snapped, "I wish—" and then caught herself. She stayed frozen like that for several seconds, and then the tears started and she ran from the kitchen.

"What did I say?" I said to nobody.

I got up and walked from the kitchen, intending to go to the bedroom and talk to her, but just then the phone rang. I detoured to the instrument and picked it up.

"Yeah, hello," I snapped.

"Did I call at a bad time?" Hocus asked.

"I assume you were there," I told him.

He laughed and said, "Couldn't see us, huh?"

"As long as you saw me I'm satisfied," I countered.

"Every step of the way," he assured me. "I got the okay all around," he said then, "so we've got the Forum for tonight."

"Good. I'll tell Trelayne when he calls me later."

"Can we count on him?" he asked.

"Hey, he's the one whose balls are in a vise," I reminded him. "He'll be there."

"Okay. Here's how it will work. The door on the Eighth Avenue side will be left unlocked. We'll all get in that way."

"Just make sure you're there. I'll be terribly disappointed if you don't make the party."

"You hold up your end, and we'll hold up ours. Uh, are you gonna bring that gun?"

"Yes," I said straight out without hedging.

"Yeah, well, if you have to fire it, watch where you're firing, huh?"

"I've fired a gun before, Hocus," I told him, not bothering to add that it was about two years ago when Eddie had been trying to get me to qualify.

"Yeah, well just watch it. Okay?"

"Yeah, sure."

"Okay, what time are you going to set this thing up for?" he asked.

Here came the lie.

"Nine-thirty," I told him. "And don't be funny, okay?" I added hurriedly, to make it sound good. "Like waiting a little extra? I don't relish taking this guy on again."

"Don't worry," he told me, "the timing is going to be just right."

"See you tonight," I told him.

I hung up the phone and found Julie staring at me. I hadn't heard her come back into the room.

"I thought you said it was going to be at nine," she said.

"Did I?" I asked. "I must have made a mistake."

"Yeah," she said, staring at me hard, "a big one."

CHAPTER FIFTY-ONE

The sex was very good, but it was also very desperate.

Again, we agreed on something without even speaking to each other. She went back into the bedroom and I followed. She had dropped the robe to the floor and was waiting for me by the bed. She was so incredibly lovely that she took my breath away, and touching her, kissing her, was just like dying and going to heaven.

When it was over we lay there side by side, catching our breath and holding hands.

"I'm so scared," she told me.

"I know. I am, too."

"This has become so much more than I ever thought it would," she told me, and I wasn't sure if she meant the problem we were facing that began with Benny's arrest or the relationship between us.

"It'll be over soon," I promised.

"Yes, but will you be alive when it is?"

I rolled on my side and looked down at her lovely face, clouded with fear and told her, "I'll be alive. I've got a lot to live for, you know?"

"What about Benny?" she asked.

"I'm still hoping to prove him innocent," I told her.

"But what will we do when he gets out?"

"We'll talk to him, Julie. That's all we can do."

"I don't want to hurt him, Jack, but I love you, and I'm·

afraid of losing you," she told me. She threw her arms around me and I cradled her sleek, firm body in my arms while she cried. She cried because she was afraid of hurting Benny and afraid that I'd get hurt—or worse.

Benny would have to understand that we never meant for this to happen.

And Max the Ax would have to understand that there was no way in hell I was going to let him do me any further harm, not while I had this woman waiting for me to come back in one piece.

CHAPTER FIFTY-TWO

It was odd being in the Forum when the lights weren't all on and the seats weren't all filled. I had a definite "ghost town" type of feeling, which didn't help my nerves any.

The Eighth Avenue door—just off Thirty-third Street—had been left unlocked as promised, and I had apparently been the first to arrive—unless the Ax was somewhere up in the seats. The only light that had been left on was shining a beacon down on the boxing ring. It would have been impossible for me to see the killer, even if he were sitting in one of those seats.

I had been referring to Max Collins several different ways: as the Ax, as Max, as the hit man; but what he was was a killer, and that's how I thought of him now. As long as I kept telling myself that he was a killer, I was sure to act with the proper caution and not try anything heroic.

I stayed by the entrance to the Thirty-third Street runway, not wanting to get near the ring, in case the killer was waiting to catch a glimpse of me. I didn't think he'd pull anything until Trelayne showed up, but I didn't want him locating me, nevertheless.

I was there about fifteen minutes when I started to worry about the others not showing up. What if the killer had followed Trelayne instead of me from Grand Central Station and had already killed him? What if he was waiting by the Eighth Avenue door to take care of Trelayne right there when he tried to get in?

I put my hand up to my head, and when I encountered the bandage over my eye it occurred to me that a flash of white at the wrong time could cost me my life. I pulled the bandage off, and as it nestled in my hand something else occurred to me, too . . .

I dropped the bandage to the floor as I heard a sound from behind me. It was a door, first opening, then closing, followed by the sound of hesitant footsteps.

I flattened myself against the door to a maintenance closet and waited to see who it was. As the footfalls got closer, I reached inside my jacket and came out with the nine-shot automatic.

The light shining down on the ring also made for a certain amount of light coming through the doorway and into the tunnel I was in. There was just enough so that I'd be able to recognize who was approaching once he came from the shadows into that dim shaft of light.

As the man who called himself Trelayne came into view, I stepped from the doorway and allowed him to see me and the gun. His eyes widened and his mouth opened as if to yell. I clamped one hand over his mouth and prodded his temple with the gun I was holding in my other hand.

"When I take my hand away," I told him, "if you make one sound I'll blow what little brains you have away. You got it?"

He gave me a panicky nod and I removed my hand.

"Jesus Christ, Jacoby, what the hell is wrong with—" he began, but he clammed up when I prodded him with the gun again.

"If you want to talk," I told him, "I'd advise you to keep it under a whisper."

"Are you crazy?" he whispered desperately.

"No, as a matter of fact I've just come to my senses," I told him.

"What are you talking about?"

"I'm talking about you, pal. I don't know what your real name is, but it sure as hell isn't Trelayne. In fact, I don't even think I've heard from the real Trelayne after that first call."

"You're crazy," he said again, obviously unable to think of anything else to say.

"No, I'm right," I told him. "I should have seen it when you called me and we set up the meet at Grand Central Station. You asked me how you would know me? Well, the real Trelayne didn't ask me that because he had been at my fight and he knew what I looked like. No, you're a phony and your job was to lure me somewhere so the man from Detroit could take me out. He must be afraid I'll find the real Trelayne first, so he figures to get me out of the way and eliminate the problem. Well," I added, prodding him with the gun again, harder, "this time I'm going to eliminate him—and you, too, if you don't do just what I tell you to do."

He flinched from the pressure of the gun and said, "W-what do you w-want me to do?"

"Tell me what the plan is?"

"I-I'm supposed to make some noise, you know, to tell him where we are. The next move was his."

"Does he have a gun?"

"Shit, no, man, he's a blade man."

"Now the rest of it," I told him, poking him hard in the temple with my iron finger.

"Man!" he protested.

"This guy's a pro, pal," I said. "We both know he's got to have a backup plan."

His shoulders slumped and he said, "I was to try to get you out by the ring."

"And he'd take it from there, right?"

"Yeah, right."

Remember, I told myself, this guy's a killer, but I went ahead and did it anyway.

The ring was my turf, not his. If he wanted to challenge me out there, who was I to turn him down? Besides, once I drew him out into the open, Hocus and his partner would close in, anyway.

"Okay, pal," I told the bogus Trelayne, "you're going to walk me out to the ring and stay ahead of me all the way. Make a move I don't like and I'll put a hole in you. Got it?"

"I got it."

"Let's go."

I took the gun away from his temple and pushed him ahead of me. I put the automatic away in the holster and started after him. I knew that if he decided to take off I wasn't about to shoot him in the back, but he didn't know it. He wasn't the one I wanted, anyway. Besides that, if he took off he wouldn't get past the cops.

As we approached the ring he started to slow down and I told him, "Keep going, friend."

"That's far enough, friend," a voice said from behind me.

I was about to turn when I felt a point of cold steel touch the side of my neck.

Shit! He must have had me spotted the whole way! And I walked right into his lap.

"Get going, Pop," the voice told the old man, and the phony man-from-the-fifth-row didn't waste any time, he just took off.

"This was a dumb play," I told the man behind me. I assumed he was Max the Ax from Detroit. "The cops are all over the place."

"You mean they were supposed to be," he told me, reaching around me and taking the gun from my holster. The knife didn't move from my neck.

I didn't like the way he sounded, much too confident. The old man was his plant, which meant that he knew this was supposed to be a trap, but he came anyway.

"You know," he told me, "personally I don't think you're worth shit, but my principal, he thinks you could be trouble, so he wanted me to take you out. As far as I'm concerned, you're just an amateur, and not even a talented one, at that."

"So go ahead," I told him, "take me out . . . from behind. So far you've killed a helpless junkie, an old man, and a woman," I told him, referring to Lucas Pratt, Corky Purcell and Louise, the black hooker. "Killing me from behind ought to be right up your alley."

"I don't have to take care of you from behind, punk," he told me, and as soon as I felt the point of the knife move away I lunged forward, beneath the bottom rope and into the ring.

I stood up and backed away to the center of the ring, wondering if he'd decide to use my gun.

"And what about the private eye you killed?" I asked him. "What about him? Did you kill him from behind, too? How come you didn't use your knife on him, huh? C'mon, big man, come on into the ring and get me, or are you afraid to face someone who's facing you?"

I was so scared my knees were threatening to start shaking, but I hoped he couldn't see it.

He stood there with my gun in one hand and his knife in the other, his face turning red as I taunted him. I was finally getting a good look at him, and he didn't look like the cold-blooded killer I knew him to be. He was about five nine, with glasses, short-cut brown hair and a brown mustache. He looked like a college professor, not a killer.

"C'mon, man," I called to him. "As far as I'm concerned,

you don't look like a hell of a lot, either. You didn't do all that great that night under the West Side Highway, did you? I fired one shot in the air and you took off like a scared rabbit. And at the gym you didn't even have the guts to make a try for me, although you were brave enough to torture an old man. C'mon, make up your mind," I shouted, wishing he'd either use the gun or throw it away.

He stared at me with ice-cold eyes and finally made his decision. The hand holding the gun began to move, and for a moment I thought he was going to use it on me; but that wasn't his intention. He held it up for me to see, then threw it away into the seats.

"I don't need a gun to handle you, friend," he told me. He approached the ring, jumped up on the apron and climbed between the ropes.

I was about to fight the biggest match of my life.

We both assumed our stances, me with my left out, he in a crouch with the knife held steady in front of him. I began to circle and he began to stalk me. I thought I needed the psychological edge of striking first, so I threw a left jab that caught him on the jaw, startling him but not doing much damage. Hell, it didn't even knock his glasses off.

I kept circling and he didn't know how to cut the ring off on me, so he just kept following me. I threw a few more tentative jabs, trying to set him up for a right. I didn't want to throw the right until I knew I could do some damage, because I knew that as soon as I threw it the stitches on my right side were likely to bust wide open.

He kept the same grim expression on his face the whole time, and his eyes never left mine. He was content to let me jab, and didn't try for me once during the first few minutes. It scared me to think that maybe he was just playing with me.

We must have circled that way, me jabbing and he just keeping up the constant pressure, for the equivalent of three rounds, only I was used to having a full minute of rest between rounds. Also, I'd been eating kind of good the last week or so, and it had started to catch up with me. He must have been in pretty damn good shape, because he wasn't even breathing hard, while my chest was starting to burn a little from the effort. I knew something was going to have to happen real soon, or he was going to be able to cut me up at his leisure.

And where the hell was Hocus? What was he doing? Sitting up in the stands eating popcorn and enjoying the fight?

I decided to take a chance. The next jab I threw I stepped in a little closer to make it more solid. It connected, but he dropped his head and took it on his forehead, at the same time slashing at me for the first time with the knife. The tip of his blade tore into my left forearm and opened a three-inch gash which started to bleed freely. I jumped back out of his range to assess the damage and also the effectiveness of my blow.

As I jumped back, he was juggling with his glasses and managed to keep them in place on his face; but until he had the glasses securely in place on his nose, for that moment his face had lost its stony composure. There was a welt on his forehead where my blow had landed, but the blow he had struck was by far the most telling. The blood was dripping to the canvas, and if I tried to use my right hand to staunch the flow, I'd be fighting one-handed. I decided to try and ignore the burning pain on my left forearm and concentrate on the fight at hand.

I decided to take advantage—or try to take advantage—of the one and only weakness I had detected during the fifteen minutes or so we had been in the ring. I stopped circling and began to back myself into one of the corners. Something was going to give this time, one way or the other, because I was trying to lure him into the corner. If my plan didn't work, then I'd be trapped in the corner, at the mercy of his blade.

A wolfish grin began to form on his mouth. He must have assumed that I was too tired to keep circling and that once he had me in the corner I was all his.

When I felt the ropes against my back I tried to look like I was totally exhausted, which didn't take a whole lot of acting. The sweat was running down my face and off my chin like a faucet. I allowed my knees to buckle a little, then took a deep breath and dropped my hands, just enough to suck him in. It took him a split second to decide to go for the kill as my hands dropped. During that split second I threw a vicious right that caught him coming in.

A few things happened at once.

First, my stitches went. I felt the pull and then the pain as they came apart, and I could feel the blood soaking through my shirt.

The effect that the blow had on him, however, made up for the pain it caused me. He took a good punch, there was no denying that, because instead of going down he staggered back a few feet, shaking his head. The desired effect, though, had

230

been achieved, because his glasses had gone sailing off and out of the ring.

It wasn't until he stopped shaking his head that he discovered what had happened, and that grim look on his face dissolved into one of panic.

He couldn't see me without his glasses!

"My glasses," he shouted, "where are my glasses? You bastard! My glasses!" he kept shouting. He was slashing about the ring with his knife, but he wasn't even close to me. I leaned against the ropes and tried to stop myself from bleeding, but I didn't know what to grab first, my arm or my side.

"Jacoby!" a voice called, and I peered out into the shadows and tried to pick up who it was. I spotted Hocus coming down an aisle, followed by his partner, Wright, and some uniformed police.

"Where the fuck were you?" I demanded, yelling it out.

Hocus motioned to the uniformed cops, who went into the ring and had no trouble subduing and disarming Max the Ax.

Hocus got up on the ring apron, and when he was right next to me I asked again, "Where the fuck were you?"

"Where the fuck was I?" he demanded angrily. "If I had listened to you, goddamnit, you'd be dead by now!" he shot back at me.

His face was beet red and the cords on his neck were standing out.

"This is just what I was afraid of," he told me. "You decided to make a grandstand play, and you almost got yourself and the old man killed! If we hadn't gotten an anonymous call telling us—"

"The old man," I repeated, starting to feel light-headed. "Did you get the old man?"

"Trelayne? Yeah, on the way out. Where the hell was he running?"

"He's not Trelayne," I told him.

"He's not? Who the hell is he, then? You told me he was—"

"Yeah, I know. Look, can we save this until later? I'm bleeding to death here, in case you didn't notice."

He looked at me without sympathy and said, "Yeah, so you are. I wonder whose fault that is?"

He grabbed my arm to help me out of the ring and said,

231

"C'mon, I've got an ambulance waiting outside. I figured you'd need one."

"That's what I like," I told him, "a vote of confidence."

With him holding my arm I jumped down off the ring apron, and then I just kept on falling...

CHAPTER FIFTY-THREE

... until I woke up in the emergency room.

I had been patched up again, and when they saw I was awake they tried to talk me into staying overnight.

"Not on your life," I told the doc, sitting up.

"No," he agreed, "but maybe on yours."

I looked at Hocus and said, "Did you take the Ax and the phony Trelayne to the precinct?" as the doctor gave me a shot of something.

"Yeah, they're holding them until I get there to talk to them."

"Well, that's where I'm going, too," I told him, sliding off the table. "I'm going to be in on the close of this."

Hocus looked at the doctor and shrugged, then held my arm while we walked out to his car.

At the precinct they let me sit in on the interrogation of both men, provided I kept my mouth shut. I was too exhausted and doped up to do much of anything else.

They talked to Max the Ax first. His composure had returned because he had his glasses back on, and he was too much of a pro to tell them much of anything. They questioned him on Lucas Pratt, Corky Purcell and the hooker, but he didn't say a word. It was only when they told him that Willy Wells was still alive and would identify him that he looked a little annoyed, but beyond that he gave them nothing.

"Ask him about Eddie," I told Hocus.

Hocus looked at me sadly, as if to say, "Reaching again," but he went ahead and threw some questions at Max the Ax about Eddie Waters, and got nothing more than he'd given up on the other three.

"Take him out," Hocus told a uniformed officer.

When Collins was out of the room I said, "It had to have been him."

"Jacoby—" Hocus began, but then he stopped and waved his hand as if to say "The hell with it."

He turned to an officer standing by the door and told him, "Bring the old man in."

The old man was a different story. He was only too willing to talk, saying that he didn't have anything to do with the murders, that was all the other guy's doing. He was only supposed to call me and arrange a meeting. When that fell through they made him call again, a call that had resulted in the Grand Central meeting.

"All I did was make some phone calls, fellas, that's all. I'm no hit man, I'm no killer," he told us desperately.

Voices started fading in and out as Hocus continued his questioning of the old man. Whatever the doctor had given me was really doing a number on me and, at one point, I think I even dozed off in my seat.

"What's your connection with this whole thing?" I heard Hocus ask him.

"Nothing, that's what I'm trying to tell ya. I ain't got no personal connection with any of this. I was just doing a job."

"For who?" I asked. The funny thing was, even as I asked the question I thought I knew the answer. It was as if I had slept for a few moments and saw the answer in a dream.

The man behind the whole thing, the man who had brought Max Collins in from Detroit, had to be somebody connected with boxing, somebody who knew I was looking for the man in the fifth row, somebody who knew me and knew where to find me, where to call me on the phone.

That's why I wasn't all that surprised when the old man looked at me and said, "Dick Gallaghen."

CHAPTER FIFTY-FOUR

The decision was made to wait until morning, when Gallaghen was in his office, before we went over to see him. Hocus had somebody drive me home, a ride I remembered nothing about when I woke up the following morning.

Julie didn't know whether to be nice to me because I was still alive, or pissed at me for getting myself cut up again and then not calling her.

When she found out that I had no intentions of staying in bed and was going out again as soon as I woke up, she decided to go ahead and be pissed.

"It's almost over, Julie," I told her.

"Well go ahead, then," she told me, "get it over with and then come back."

I went downstairs and found Hocus waiting for me in his car.

"You're late," he told me.

I couldn't remember our having made an appointment for him to pick me up, but I got in and said, "Sorry, I overslept."

"He overslept, he says," he muttered, starting the car. "You wouldn't leave the station house last night until I promised to pick you up this morning, and now you tell me you overslept."

"Must have been that shit the doctor shot me up with," I told him.

"Sure. Here," he said, handing me my gun from his pocket. "We picked it up last night." I took it and put it in my pocket.

"How do you intend to play this?" I asked him.

He started to answer, then looked at me and said, "I've got a feeling that you want to suggest something."

"Yeah, I do. Let me go in ahead of you. You can stay out in the front office and keep Gallaghen's secretary from buzzing him. When I get inside his office I'll switch on his intercom, and you'll be able to hear everything that's said."

He thought it over, then shrugged and said, "Sounds okay. My partner's bringing the old man with him, so if you can't crack him we can bring him in and that might do it."

"Okay."

I put my head back and let the sun bake my eyes, which felt gritty, and asked, "Did you talk to Max the Ax again after I left?"

He shot a glance over at me again, and then said, "Yeah, I did."

"Did he say anything about killing Eddie Waters?"

"Kid, he didn't say anything about anything. The man's a pro. He's not about to talk."

"It had to be him," I said with my eyes closed.

"You've got to prove it, kid," he told me, "not pray for it."

He was right about that. The only way to get Benny out of jail for murder was to prove he didn't do it, and so far I hadn't even come close.

We rode the rest of the way in silence, and when we reached Gallaghen's building Hocus parked his car next to a hydrant and we went up. We found Wright, Hocus's partner, waiting for us with the phony Trelayne in front of Gallaghen's door.

"You get a name on him yet?" I asked, indicating the old man.

Hocus shook his head.

"He's been talkative about everything but that," he told me.

"He still thinks he's got a chance of being let go," Wright added.

The old guy threw Wright a hurt look and then threw Hocus a hopeful one.

"Get inside," Hocus told him, opening the door and pushing him in. We all followed.

Patrice looked up from her desk, frowning until she saw me.

"Hi, Jack. What's all this?" she asked.

"Just don't touch your intercom, little lady," Hocus told her, showing her his shield and ID.

"Police," she said. "I don't understand." She looked at me and asked again, "What's going on?"

"I think if you're patient, Pat, you'll find out," I told her. "I'd like you to do me a very big favor, okay? I promise you'll understand in a few minutes."

"What do you want me to do?" she asked.

"I want you to buzz Dick and tell him that I'm here. Don't mention the fact that anyone else is here."

"Jack, what—"

"This is important, Pat," I told her.

I was hoping Hocus wouldn't try to push her, because then I thought she'd balk. Luckily he kept quiet, and she decided to go along.

"All right, Jack." She depressed the proper button, and when Gallaghen answered she announced, "Miles Jacoby is here to see you, sir."

There was a long beat of silence as he adjusted himself to the fact that I wasn't dead, that I hadn't been killed the night before by his hit man.

"Well, send him in, Pat," he finally told her. She turned off the intercom, looked at me and shrugged.

"Thanks," I told her. "Shouldn't take me more than a few seconds to switch on the intercom," I told Hocus.

He nodded, and I went over and knocked on Gallaghen's door.

"Come ahead," he called out.

I opened the door and walked in.

"Hello, Dick," I said to the man who was my last chance to prove my brother innocent of murder.

"Hi, Jack."

I approached his desk and took his outstretched hand. As I shook hands with him with my right hand, I hit the "on" switch on his intercom with my left, saying, "How are you?" to cover the small click it made.

"I'm fine, my boy, but you look a little worse for wear."

"Yeah, well, that guy you hired has been giving me kind of a hard time these past few days, but that's all settled now," I told him, deciding to get right down to it.

He frowned and said, "What guy? What are you talking about, Jack?"

"Oh, come off it, Dick," I said, sitting down. "You must have known I'd put the whole thing together sooner or later."

He took time to light one of his smelly Turkish cigarettes,

also using the time to think. Should he waste the breath it would take to deny it, he was probably thinking. Finally he planted his right forefinger along his right cheek and said thoughtfully, "Actually, I was never quite sure whether you would or you wouldn't, Jack. I've watched you fight for three years now, and I always thought that you could have been a good one if you'd put your heart into it. The problem was, you never did. So I thought, what happens now that he wants to play detective? Well, I figure maybe you'll want to put your heart into that. You're a smart young man, Jack, so I figured if we kept an eye on you, maybe you'd lead us to Trelayne."

"How did you know that the man I was looking for was Trelayne?" I asked.

"I got a call from someone who thought the information might be worth money. His name is not important; he was just somebody who hung around. He told me that Trelayne was going to be at the fight that night. I called some friends of mine in Detroit and asked that they send me someone who could, ah, take care of him for me. They sent me this fellow Max the Ax—can you imagine such a name? He assured me that he would take care of Trelayne that night."

"But he didn't."

Gallaghen gave a great sigh and said, "No, he did not. In fact, after the fight he lost him completely. I was able to find out whose ticket he used to get in, and I gave Mr. 'Ax' the information before I gave it to you."

"Why did you give it to me at all?" I asked.

"Could I have refused without arousing your suspicions?" he asked me. "Obviously that information was available to me since I promoted the fight. I could not refuse you, Jack; all I could do was make sure my man got there first."

"And he killed Purcell without finding out where Trelayne was," I finished.

Again he sighed, which had always been his way of showing his displeasure.

"The man was a lout," he told me. "Not a skilled interrogator, but a killer. He decided to torture the old man for the information, and the old man died before he could tell my man where Trelayne was."

"And even if he had told him where Trelayne was, he would have killed him anyway, to keep me from talking to him."

"I imagine."

"Was he supposed to kill me, too?" I asked.

238

"No, no, my boy, I never wanted that. The night under the highway you merely surprised him, and he lashed out in self-defense. He had strict orders that no harm was to come to you. That was insisted upon by——" he started to say, but then stopped, as if he realized he was saying too much.

"By who, Dick?" I asked.

"Why, by me, of course, my boy. I've always been very fond of you, you know."

I let it go, even though I knew he was holding something back.

"Okay, so if he wasn't supposed to kill me, why lure me to the Felt Forum?" I asked.

Another sigh, after which he said, "I'm afraid the man panicked. You see, you had seen him twice now. Once at the hotel where Purcell was staying and once under the highway."

"I didn't get a good look at him either time," I told him.

"Yes, but he had no way of knowing that. Then he became aware that you were after him, as well as looking for Trelayne."

"Who told him that?" I asked.

He merely shrugged and raised his hands.

"I assume the man has his own connections," was all he'd say, but I felt that, once again, he was lying.

"What about those mugs on the street?" I asked.

"They were only supposed to warn you off," he said after another obligatory sigh. "Unfortunately, you did not give them a chance."

"And Lucas Pratt?"

"That was not my idea," he sighed. "I did hire the man, but he did not clear his methods through me."

No, that would have been all Max's idea, all right. He must have known Lucas was a junkie, and whether he killed him deliberately or Lucas just died on him the way Purcell did, he had to make it look like an accident. As far as Gallaghen was concerned, he couldn't avoid all the blame for Lucas's death. Max had to have gotten Lucas's name from someone, and Dick fit the bill.

With Purcell, Max obviously didn't have time to set up an accident, because I practically walked in on him and he had to get away. He and whoever he was with had left. It had probably just been a small-time hood he was using as a bird dog, since he didn't know New York all that well. He'd probably discarded the guy when he was of no further use—one way or another.

How he spotted Louise, the black hooker, was anybody's

guess. Maybe she even got brave and tried to hit him up for a payoff. Who knew? Once he knew about her, though, she had to go.

But Eddie, what about Eddie?

"Dick, what about Eddie?"

He paused a moment to crush out his cigarette and then took the time to light up another.

"Your brother, he's going to get convicted, isn't he?" Dick asked.

"It looks that way, Dick," I told him, "unless I can prove he didn't do it."

Shaking his head, he said, "I can't help you prove it, Jack. In fact, this whole conversation is just your word against mine, otherwise I wouldn't be talking to you."

I forced myself to look right into his eyes.

"For your own peace of mind, however, I will tell you that your brother is innocent."

It took a monumental effort for me to remain in my chair. I wanted to jump to that intercom and yell at Hocus, "See, you dumb cop?"

"Who killed him, Dick?"

"It was this fellow, Max the Ax," he told me. "I, ah, learned that your brother was on his way to see Eddie and that he was drunk. I sent my man there ahead of him. He waited outside the office, and when the secretary came running out he went in. Your brother was actually so drunk, Jack, that he blundered past my man without even seeing him."

I believed that. It wasn't the first time Benny had gotten blind drunk.

"When my man went into Eddie's office, he found him unconscious. Your brother had indeed given him a fearful beating, Jack, but he didn't kill him. My man took care of that, and then he just waited for the police to find Benny wandering around the building. After they left with your brother, my man simply walked away from the scene."

"Where is Max the Ax, by the way? Did you kill him?"

I shook my head.

"He's in custody, Dick, and so is the man you—or he—had impersonating Trelayne." I leaned forward in my chair and asked him, "Is there really a Trelayne, Dick?"

He crushed out his second cigarette viciously and said, "Oh yes, my boy, he is real. He was real twenty years ago, and he's real now. He's still out there, somewhere, and he's real—and I am going to get him, one day."

"Dick, it's all over."

He shook his head.

"It will never be over, Jack. I don't forget my family that easy, not even after twenty years. If it takes another twenty years, this man will surface again. and I'll find him and pay him back."

I looked at Dick Gallaghen, and even allowing for the extra weight, which made guessing his age correctly difficult, he still wasn't old enough to have been the dead boxer's father.

Yet, he had mentioned "family."

"Dick, what is this obsession you have with Trelayne?" I asked him.

"You know the story by now, Jack. You must."

"I know about a young boxer who was killed when Trelayne refused to let his man go in the tank. Those things happen, Dick. That's boxing."

He shook his head.

"Those things don't happen to Ray Gallaghen," he said through his teeth. I had never seen Dick Gallaghen so passionate about anything before.

"Was that the boxer's name?" I asked.

He nodded.

"And then his father had the other boxer killed?"

He nodded again.

"He let some people he worked for know that he wanted that to happen," he told me, "and it did."

"And what about Trelayne?"

"Trelayne knew that he was next on the list, and he started running. We looked for him for a while, but then those people my father worked for forgot about him. Even the old man forgot about him after a while. But I didn't forget. I never forgot, and I never will forget."

I waited for him to go on and finish, and when he did he explained it all.

"You don't forget your only baby brother."

CHAPTER FIFTY-FIVE

Johnny Ricardi punched the shit out of me, which was possibly the best thing that could have happened to me. The ref stepped in at 1:26 of the third round and called it a draw—at least, that's what I'll tell my grandchildren.

So I retired from the ring with a 12–4 record and all of my marbles, which is more than I can say for a lot of ex-pugs.

Like Packy, who was just setting another beer down in front of me.

"Packy, you ever think that maybe you retired a few fights too late?" I asked him.

"Sure I did, Jack," he answered. "That's why I jump at shadows and still hear the bell for the fifteenth round once in a while. I'm glad you're getting out early, Kid. There's a lot of things you could do."

"Sure, Packy. Thanks."

A lot of things I could do, he said. Sure. Should I tell him what I had, now that my ring career was over? I had just been thinking about that a few hours ago, in the offices of Waters & Jacoby, Private Investigators, when Missy buzzed me and told me that Detective Hocus was there to see me.

"Send him in, Missy," I told her.

Hocus came in and sat down, wincing at what Johnny Ricardi had done to my face.

"Some things never change, huh?" he asked.

"Some things do," I countered, pointing to the wall where I'd hung up my gloves.

"You're going to do this for a living from now on?" he asked.

"That's right."

"You're crazy. This is almost as bad as police work."

I shrugged and said, "A man's got to eat."

"I guess so," he agreed.

There was an awkward kind of silence for a few seconds, and then he said, "I understand your brother's coming home today."

"About time, too," I told him.

"Ah, red tape, technicalities," he said. "At least he's getting out—and he's dry."

"That won't last long," I said.

He didn't say anything to that.

"What about the others?" I asked.

"Well, with Willy Wells's testimony, and the old man—"

"Who was that old man, anyway?" I interrupted.

"He was just hired to make calls and then meet you at Grand Central. With his testimony as well, we got Max the Ax put away for a while."

"What's a while?"

"Well, we couldn't really get him on murder." He ticked them off on his fingers. "Nobody saw him do the junkie, the hooker, or the old man in the hotel. You can't identify him because you didn't get a good look at the man in the hotel or under the highway."

"What about his assaulting me at the Forum? Don't you need me to testify—"

He shook his head and waved me off.

"That wouldn't have added significantly to his sentence," he told me. "You assaulted him, too, if you remember."

"In self-defense."

"Or vice versa. Better not to even bring it up," he assured me.

"What about Dick Gallaghen."

"We've got him on some conspiracy charges. He's confessed to hiring Max the Ax to find and kill Trelayne but insists he knows nothing about the other murders. He'll be away for a while, too."

"And the real Trelayne is still out there, running."

"The real one never called you after that first time?"

244

I shook my head.

"He must have gotten to the West Side Highway late, but in time to see Max the Ax. After that he couldn't bring himself to trust me again, I guess. I wish there was some way to get word to him."

He shrugged and stood up.

"I just figured you'd like to know what was going on," he told me.

"Thanks."

"Good luck with your new business. Try and stay out of my hair, okay?"

"Yeah."

He looked out toward the outer office, where Missy was, and said, "Well, at least you've got a good-looking secretary."

"Yeah, thanks."

When he left I put my feet up on the desk and stared at the ceiling. Eddie was gone, my boxing career was gone, Benny was coming home, but would we ever really be brothers again?

And then there was Julie, who, as I had discovered, was not what she pretended to be. I had been about to get up and leave the office to go and see her when Missy came in.

"Jack?" she called from the door. I dropped my feet and sat up.

"Yes, Missy?"

She came into the room carrying her purse, which I thought was odd since it wasn't even noon yet.

"Jack, I can't stay anymore," she told me. "I hope you understand. There's just too much of Eddie here."

"I understand, Missy," I told her. "You go ahead."

"I put the files in order, Jack—what's left of them."

"What is left of them, Missy?" I asked.

"Not much, Jack. What you've got left are a lot of closed cases. It took you too long to decide to keep the office open. Even the regular retainers have gone elsewhere."

"Well, I guess I'll just have to build up my own clients' list, won't I?"

"Good luck, Jack—and I'm sorry."

"Don't be sorry, Missy. Just remember where to come if you ever need anything."

"I'll remember," she promised. "Bye."

I looked over at the wall where I had hung up my gloves that morning. An office and a pair of old boxing gloves—that was all I had.

And then again, I thought of Julie. I guess she could have been mine, if I could ignore the facts that had presented themselves to me when I had really sat down and thought the whole affair over. As a result of that, I knew that she would never be mine.

I also knew that she would never again be Benny's either.

I signaled Packy for another beer and thought over my last meeting with Julie, which had been a scant half hour ago.

I had left my office and gone straight to her apartment. I wanted to get there ahead of Benny, and I wanted to get her out of there before he got home.

"Jack," she said breathlessly when she answered the door. She tried to put her arms around me, but I couldn't afford that. If I had let her, then I might have changed my mind.

She looked at me, puzzled, but she said, "I'm glad you're here, darling, we can tell Benny together."

"I'm here, all right, but you won't be for very long. Pack a bag, Julie. I don't want you to be here when Benny comes home."

"Oh, darling, I think we should tell him together—"

"I'll tell him everything he needs to know," I assured her, "like what a cheap, two-timing, conniving bitch he married."

"Miles!"

"Don't look so shocked, Julie. You probably didn't think I would be smart enough to figure it out, but I did. Part of it, anyway. You're going to explain the rest."

"Miles, I—"

"Let's go," I said, taking her arm and leading her to the bedroom. "I'll tell you what I figured out while you pack, then you can tell me the rest."

I got a bag out of her closet for her and put it on the bed, open.

"Start packing."

She looked at me helplessly, then began to throw odd pieces of clothing into it while I talked.

"The big thing I couldn't understand was how Max the Ax could have been waiting for me under the West Side Highway that night. I knew he hadn't followed me, and I'd assumed that he followed the real Trelayne. But the real Trelayne had got there late, and Max was already there. He'd gotten there ahead of both of us. Now, I'd told only one person about that meeting, the only person I thought I could trust—you! Don't try and tell me I'm wrong, Julie. I even sensed, while I was talking to Dick Gallaghen, that he was protecting someone. A couple of times he almost gave it away, but he caught himself. He had been about to tell me at one point that someone had demanded that I not be hurt. That would have been you, too. Keep packing," I snapped as she turned to face me, "and tell me why. Tell me why Eddie Waters had to be killed. What did he have to do with it all?"

After Gallaghen had been taken into custody by Hocus at his office, I had asked him that same question, and he'd refused to answer. Now I'd find out why.

"C'mon!" I shouted, and she jumped.

"Miles, I love you—" she started, with tears in her eyes.

"That's bullshit!"

"It's true!" she shouted at me. "I love you and I hate Benny!"

"That's why Eddie had to be killed?" I demanded. "You're not making sense, Julie."

"All right!" she shouted. Then again, quietly, she said, "All right. The—the day that Benny went to see Eddie, I saw him at Packy's. He never mentioned it, but I saw him outside and he told me where he was going."

If that was true, Benny had probably never mentioned it because he didn't remember.

"I knew where he was going, and I called Dick and told him."

"Why Dick?"

"He had called me, after you went to see him. He—he wanted me to help him keep tabs on you while you were looking for Trelayne. At first I said no, but then when Benny told me where he was going, I saw a way out. I saw a way to get rid of Benny so I could be with you."

"Keep going!" I told her.

"You know what happened. Benny beat Eddie up, and then Dick's man went in and killed him. Benny would be convicted of Eddie's killing, and I'd divorce him and marry you. Benny would never give me a divorce otherwise. I knew that."

"So you helped frame Benny?"

"I did it so I could be with you."

"With me?" I asked. "You disgust me, Julie! You did that to my brother, to be with me?"

"I never thought you'd find out," she explained.

"So you agreed to help Dick if he would help frame Benny. That's why you called him and told him I'd be meeting Trelayne under the bridge."

"Yes."

"You almost got me killed, Julie," I reminded her.

"That wasn't supposed to happen, Miles, I swear."

"And what about the Felt Forum? That wasn't supposed to happen either?"

"I saved your life at the Felt Forum!" she shouted. "When I knew that you were going there half an hour before the police, I called Hocus and told him."

I remembered Hocus saying something about getting there in time because of an anonymous phone call, but I'd never let him finish.

"That doesn't excuse everything else you've done," I told her. "And it doesn't explain it all. Why the hell did Dick Gallaghen think that you would help him in the first place?"

Her shoulders slumped, and she sat on the bed.

"He knew I wanted Trelayne dead, too," she told me.

"You wanted Trelayne dead?" I asked, surprised. "What the hell connection could you have had with him?"

She tried to blink back the tears as she looked at me.

"Miles, Dick Gallaghen is my uncle."

"What? That means—"

She nodded.

"Ray Gallaghen, the boxer who was killed in the ring twenty years ago," she said, sobbing, "he was my father!"

EPILOGUE

So I let her go.

Actually, I gave her a choice. Either leave New York and never come back, or I'd tell Benny the whole story.

Turning her over to the police had never occurred to me, especially after I learned that Ray Gallaghen had been her father. Not that I condoned what she had done because of that. The simple truth was that I still loved her too much to send her to jail.

She had finished packing and without another word, without a good-bye and—above all—without our *touching* each other, she had left.

And I had come to Packy's to get roaring drunk. Later, I'd explain it to Benny, somehow.

Much later.

"You're really throwing it down tonight, Jack," Packy observed. "I thought you'd be out celebrating, what with Benny getting out and all."

"What makes you think I'm not celebrating?" I asked him.

"Jack, this is me, remember? I know the diff between celebrating drinking, and down-in-the-dumps drinking. This," he added, putting another beer down in front of me, "is down-in-the-dumps drinking."

"If you're so smart," I said to him, "tell me something."

"What?"

"There's a man out there who's running for his life and has

249

been for twenty years, and now he doesn't have to do it any-more. How do I let him know?"

"You mean Trelayne?"

"Yeah, I mean Trelayne."

"He's in the clear?" he asked, studying my face intently.

"Yeah, he's in the clear. Gallaghen's in the can, and Tre-layne's in the clear. But I don't know where the hell he is, so he's still running."

He hesitated a moment, then he said, "I know where he is."

I looked at him and asked, "You know—"

"I've known all along, Jack, but I promised not to tell."

"Well, shit," I said, putting my beer down. "Where's he been all this time?"

"Here," he said, then pointing upstairs toward his apartment he added, "my place. I'm the one who got him to call you that time, but I couldn't get him to do it again."

"Well, shit," I said again.

"I'm sorry, Jack, but I promised. See, he used to train me—"

"That's all right, Packy. You had to keep your promise. Do you know where he is now?" I asked.

"I sure do."

"Well, then you can tell him for me," I began, "tell him he can stop running."

"Tell him yourself," Packy said, pointing behind me. "He's sitting in the last booth over there."

I turned around and saw the back of a man's head. I looked back at Packy and he nodded, so I picked up my beer and walked over to meet my man from the fifth row.